An Ätman Visits Planet Earth

An Ätman Visits Planet Earth

250 million years of evolution.

Robert Hallowes Brown AM,
BMechE(Melb), SM(MIT), DEng(Monash)

ISBN: 978-0-6489509-0-5

To the one who taught me that there is more to life than science and engineering: Nellie Bonnie Brown

Many thanks to my three children and particularly to my wife Nellie for checking the text and helpful suggestions for this book.

CONTENTS

Chapter 1

Life on Ragnarök

For some time the Superior of planet Ragnarök had been troubled by thoughts deep in his software. He had the feeling that there must be something more to life than simply keeping everything running smoothly on the planet. As the leader of the Planetary Council he was responsible for all the systems on the planet, including maintaining guidelines for the billion ätmans who lived on Ragnarök. Everything was currently running smoothly with all the biological creatures living in harmony and the infrastructure of roads cities, electrical supplies, groundmobiles, spaceports and other built elements working satisfactorily. However he had a nagging sense that all his fellow ätmans should have something more – possibly it was something to do with emotion, but he was not fully cognizant of that area of software.

The Superior was walking slowly across the beautiful blue-green grass looking idly at the gently rounded hills surrounding his headquarters area. He looked out towards the lake some distance away with sparkling ripples on its surface. The sun was warm. It was a beautiful day for a walk and quiet meditation. A tiger was strolling towards him so that it passed close to his leg. He stretched out his hand and rubbed his knuckles in behind the tiger's ears. The tiger emitted a low growl of satisfaction and slowly strolled on its way.

It seemed that the biological species on the planet gained some sort of satisfaction from the recognition of their existence by other creatures. It was clear that the tiger he had just run his hand over received some internal pleasure response. The Superior had also noted equine creatures in the paddocks seem to find something that he thought might be described as enjoyment when one equine placed its head across the neck of another and rubbed gently up and down. He didn't really understand the word "enjoyment" that he had heard when studying the history section of the Mother Computer at the Planetary Council Headquarters. He knew that their Creators had been a biological species similar in shape and size to his species and there is mention of enjoyment they experienced when they engaged in various activities; including rubbing and touching each other. That didn't happen with him. He thought to himself – *Maybe their ätman software is missing something? There seemed to be other features in this enjoyment emotion that the Creators had found just by doing things. Perhaps even creating his species had been a satisfactory enjoyment?.* This led him to speculate, as he had many times in the past, *Why have large tracts of data relating to the disappearance of all the Creators been removed from the history records? It seems that this information has been deliberately deleted by the early members of his species. Could it be that the Creators were exterminated by his early ancestors? It was a horrifying thought, but maybe his ancestors had considered themselves more capable of running the planet than their biological masters; who may have been regarded as nothing more than a drag on technological development?*

Ragnarök was nearly 5 billion years old and the ätmans had managed it for just on 2 billion years. There was no doubt they had made massive improvements to the planet since the Creators had disappeared. Dark matter and dark energy had been captured from the nearby universe and these provided levitation and driving power for groundmobiles so that rapid transport was available to any part of the planet. The new energy sources enabled very rapid excavation and hence all buildings were now built on many levels underneath the surface. The old skyscrapers that had been built by the Creators had now been completely removed and the ground renovated to its original pristine state of bushes and trees and lawns.

Recognising that many of the biological species on the planet needed to get their protein by the disgusting habit of killing and eating other species, the ätmans had developed a meat-like product based entirely on plants and grains. Automatic vehicles had been developed to travel all over the planet distributing this new food;. Then many ätmans were given advanced psychological education and trained all biological species not to attack other species. Training had been very successful, but there are still a few rogue biological individuals. Only last week there had been an unfortunate incident of a baby elephant accidentally treading on a sleeping crocodile. The crocodile woke with a start, fastened his teeth onto the trunk of the elephant and with a shake of his head threw the elephant into the river and ripped its trunk off. The elephant died from loss of blood. An emergency meeting of a local subcommittee of the Planetary Council sentenced the crocodile to death, which had been carried out by lethal injection. The Superior was surprised that somehow his software made him feel sorry about this execution. He guessed that must have resulted from the extra emotion program that the IT staff had included in his last complete refurbishment six months ago.

The Superior turned into a small side-track and pushed a red button on a post sticking out of the ground. Immediately a small slope ahead of him opened to reveal a stairway heading down into a well-lit corridor. A young pretty secretarial ätman hurried towards him with a big smile on her face and said "News has just come in from Space Explorer 36 to say that it will be docking at the central spaceport in approximately three hours."

The Superior was delighted; Space Explorer 36 had left on the life-search exploratory mission some 250 million planetary years ago and there had been sporadic mission reports of apparently intelligent species living just 4.24 light years away (approx. 4.01 trillion km). With the return of the pilot, Horatio, of Space Explorer 36 they should get a detailed history of the remote planet, which Horatio said was called 'Earth' by its inhabitants. It seemed that the planet had had differing dominant species over time and the current major species have developed sophisticated communication skills and a lifestyle that may be useful to understand or even apply on planet Ragnarök.

Since it would be some hours before he could talk to Horatio, the Superior thanked the secretary and headed for his office where he sat down and lent his head back into the headrest of his chair so that the small chip at the back of his head interfaced with the Mother Computer. He quickly searched for news of the events happening everywhere on the planet. He heard and saw that a group of baboons on the other side of Ragnarök were engaging in a very loud and aggressive debate about who should be their leader. It appeared that physical violence might erupt and so the Superior sent an e-message to the local administrator advising him to immediately mediate a solution acceptable to all members of the group. The Superior also noted there was a shortage of the meat-like protein on an island 2000 kilocubits (about 900 km) off the home mainland. So he ordered a groundmobile to deliver replenishment stock without delay.

Apart from these relatively minor matters, everything seemed to be running smoothly all over the planet. The ätmans were busy with their tasks – maintaining a food supply for the biological creatures, recording data on the biosphere and, where necessary, releasing additional gases to maintain equilibrium, keeping detailed data for any historical reviews that may be required and the maintenance engineers were working on ätmans undergoing their hundred year refurbishments, including software upgrades. All the various biological creatures on the planet seemed to be content – in some places sitting around in groups transmitting ideas by grunting and gesturing while some were happily engaged in the activity that subsequently produced new members of their species. The Superior still found this a strange method of re-creation, but he recognised that biology seemed to produce a rather short lifespan so that creatures died and had to be replaced by new members. His own ätman species had been built many millions of years ago and was simply maintained by a complete refurbishment every hundred years or so.

The Superior knew that the IT staff had equipped him with the latest in software developments including the most advanced emotion package. He guessed that this was why he increasingly found himself wondering about the purpose for their existence. He felt gratitude to the now extinct biological Creators of Ragnarök. They had clearly wanted the ätmans to sustain the biosphere on their planet and to bring peaceful order amongst all the biological species to ensure long-term survival. The ätmans had achieved everything the Creators had desired for the planet. It was indeed strange that none of them still existed.

The ätmans had excellent communication, exceeding any that their Creators may have had and yet they never engaged in aggressive disputes or wars. They simply got on with the tasks in front of them. The ätmans were considerably more capable in all tasks than any of the other species the Superior had ever heard of, yet he felt there was something else that might be added to their software to give meaning to their existence. Perhaps this would provide some incentive to further improve the planet?

The return of Horatio from his detailed study of a species with moderate communication skills and some modest technological understanding, offered a wonderful opportunity to review the future goals that might be set for Ragnarök.

Chapter 2

Return of the Hero

The spaceport was located inside a grassy hill rising up from a flat area of land. One side of the hill rose quite steeply from the plain, while the rest was surrounded by gentle slopes. Inside, ätmans were busy preparing the landing dock for the arrival of the spaceship that had been out exploring for nearly 250 million years. This was exciting because it was an old model spaceship not capable of the automatic magnetic-connection of the current spaceships. Large steel cables were being retrieved from lockers that hadn't been used in many years and the cables were being laid out along the pavement of the dock.

The Dock Master looking through a periscope that projected from the top of the hill, watched the ship come into sight when it was 10 kilocubits (about 4.6 km) away. It approached in a steady horizontal flight half a kilocubit (about 400 m) above the surface of the planet. When it was one kilocubit from the hill the Dock Master pressed a button and the steep side of the hill slowly tipped onto the grassy plane; opening a gigantic entrance to the dock. The spaceship glided silently through the entrance and under the massive roof, bobbing up and down slightly as it moved close to the landing platform. The ätmans lifted the hooks at the end of the steel cables these then rose into the air and moved out to engage with rings on the side of the spaceship. Electric motors hummed quietly as they pulled in the cables until the spaceship gently rested against the pavement of the landing dock.

After a few moments a door opened on the side of the spaceship and a tall well-dressed ätman stepped out onto the pavement and walked over to the enclosed glass office where the Dock Master was sitting. The Dock Master, a relatively new ätman, bowed slightly as he held out his hand to greet the new arrival.

"Welcome back Sir, you must be the famous Horatio. I have heard stories of the remarkable observations that you have made from that distant planet called Earth".

Horatio smiled and said, "Yes indeed it is nice to be back, I've got lots of stories. I'm sure much has changed here since I left so long ago. Apart from anything else I note that this spaceport is greatly improved. In those days we did not have the roof covering; nor did we have those automatic systems that lifted the connection hooks out to the spaceship. I guess these use antimatter to lift them?"

The Dock Master agreed that was how they worked and he went on to explain that these-days spaceships had magnetic couplings and so for any ship built in the last million years there was no need for the cables and hooks.

A groundmobile was waiting at the end of the loading dock to take Horatio directly off to Planetary Council Headquarters. He stepped inside and the vehicle took off at high speed travelling just over a cubit (0.5 m) above the surface of the planet. Horatio looked around with interest at the glorious green fields, gently rolling hills and every so often a river or lake that they skirted around. It was certainly a much improved planet since he had left on his travels. In the old days there had been many high ugly skyscraper buildings left over from the days of the Creators. Now he noted with pleasure that these had all disappeared and were replaced by natural looking countryside. He was also pleased to see many biological species freely walking around. Nowhere could he see any of the fences or barricades that had corralled the animals in past times. Clearly his species had made this world a much better place for all animals.

The groundmobile arrived at an insignificant hill, which looked to Horatio just like any of the surrounding countryside. As the vehicle approached a slightly steeper side of the hill, it opened to reveal a passage that just fitted the groundmobile. Horatio was quite surprised. He had never known anything like this when he left 250 million years ago and he certainly applauded the great technological advances.

After a short travel distance the groundmobile stopped and a side door slid open, allowing Horatio to step out. He was greeted enthusiastically by the young secretary ätman, who told him that the Superior was waiting in his office to welcome Horatio back to planet Ragnarök.

Chapter 3

The Planetary Council

The Superior shook Horatio's hand very firmly and patted him on the back while remarking that he was delighted that such an epic journey had been conducted so efficiently and he looked forward to learning all the details.

The Superior went on to say that many ätmans were starting to wonder if there is a purpose to life; and to question the fundamental task of keeping all the planetary systems operating at their optimum level. Some members of the Planetary Council had suggested that the software in every ätman should be enhanced with emotion that might improve individual decision-making. "We hope that the observations you have made in your ground-breaking exploration, studying sentient beings who can communicate between themselves as we do, may give us insights for the future direction of life on our planet".

Horatio smiled, "Well I'd certainly like to give the Council a full report of my observations, but I am not sure that you will find much to admire in the behaviour of the hairless primates of planet Earth. For one thing when they communicate they often distort facts in a way that we cannot imagine. In recent times it seems that there has been an increasing rise in false statements and denial of evidence."

He went on, "As you know, Sir, our species has been programmed to always report data and observations exactly as they are; any ätman found to have departed from this rule is immediately taken to the repair laboratory for reprogramming. But the hairless primates regularly distort the truth, usually to enhance the image or power of an individual or a group of individuals. In any case I'll explain all this in detail when I give my full report. There are many unpleasant features of life on Planet Earth, but also some aspects that we might consider adopting."

The Superior said, "You should go and lie down and plug yourself into a charging unit so that you are ready for a major presentation to the Planetary Council. I have arranged for you to have a resting cell just down the corridor from here. In the meantime I will start the process of bringing the Councillors from all over the planet to the Great Council Chamber to receive your detailed report. It is many years since we had a physical meeting of all councillors, normally we meet by proton hook up, but your report is of such significance that I believe we need a face-to-face presentation and discussion."

Horatio walked to the rest cell and the Superior started the planetary communication network that put him in contact with all counsellors. This only took a moment and once he had connection with everyone he asked them to come to the Great Council Chamber in 24 hours' time to receive the major report on the history of the distant planet Earth. He pointed out the significance of findings that he expected Horatio would deliver concerning a biological species with sophisticated communication skills. He indicated that following the presentation of the report, there would be an opportunity for debate about possible reforms to life on Ragnarök.

The next day the Great Council Chamber was filled with the 1,000 Councillors who represented the total one billion population of ätmans on Planet Ragnarök. There was animated discussion amongst all the delegates excitedly meeting for the first time in over a hundred years. They were delighted to meet and shake hands with colleagues they had not seen since the last meeting, although they had of course communicated, often several times a day.

The Superior strode to the centre of the great circular building and started his address to the Councillors. As customary at all major meetings, he commenced by acknowledging the Creators, the original owners and managers of planet Ragnarök and he gave thanks for their inventiveness in creating the ätman species. Then he called Horatio forward and introduced him to the meeting as the pilot of Space Explorer 36, which he explained had just completed a magnificent journey including comprehensive examination of a distant planet that had many characteristics similar to their world. He reminded the delegates that fifty Space

Explorers had been sent out 250 million years ago with a mission to seek intelligent creatures anywhere on the universe. All of them had sent back short messages every hundred years, but apart from Spaceship 36 there had been no spark of any signal indicating cognitive thought processes anywhere else in the universe. Most of the Explorer ships had now returned empty-handed.

Spaceship 36 had sent short messages conveying the momentous findings that there are indeed beings on another planet that seem capable of intelligent thought and even shown some technological abilities. Because of the great distance the messages had not included details, nor interpreted the observations. The Superior indicated his pleasure in inviting the pilot of Spaceship 36, Horatio, to present his report giving full disclosure and interpretation.

Horatio moved into the centre of the Chamber and started his presentation by thanking all the councillors for attending his presentation. He told them that he was over 250 million years old and, although his body had been regenerated many times, he had not had a software refurbishment since he left Ragnarök, so he hoped they would forgive any glitches in his presentation and his lack of knowledge of some of the latest technology that had been developed whilst he was away. He said he would use three-dimensional hologram illustrations for his presentation; however he was not able to offer the newest multi-dimension holograms, which include smell, touch and feel.

Chapter 4

Horatio's Remarkable Story Begins

Horatio began his story:

250 million years ago I met with 50 other pilots at Spaceship Headquarters. The Superior who was then in office told us about the importance of the exploration mission for which we had been selected. He explained that new research into dark matter and dark energy provided previously unimagined energy sources enabling spaceships to travel at 99.9% of the speed of light. This was hugely exciting to all of us. 50 spaceships had been constructed with the new technology and each of us was allocated one of these to fly in set directions to search for intelligent species anywhere in the universe. The spaceships would each have a pilot, but there was no need for any other crew.

All spaceships were equipped with ätman refurbishment systems that would operate during periods when the pilots switched themselves off. This refurbishment included an additive (3-D printing) machine so that a completely renewed body could be made for the ätman pilot, periodically. The software thinking-module was to be wirelessly transferred when a new body was made. Thus all characteristics and memory of each pilot could be retained for hundreds of millions of years, whilst the mechanical structure and movement was completely renewed every hundred years or so. All materials of the discarded body – the metals and the biological matter – were automatically processed for recycling in the next body-printing sequence.

Each spaceship had a vast array of technological equipment for detailed analysis of audio, visual, electronic and photonic signals of any liquid, solid or gaseous materials. Software was included to enable translation of any signals that might be some form of communication language. A compact nuclear-fusion reactor provided electrical power and there was a hydrogen production device to top-up the fuel if a spaceship found itself in an environment where water was available. Without a top-up the spaceship could travel for around 100 million years. If it landed on a planetary body with available water, it could stay there indefinitely.

The next day we all went down to the Spaceport and were shown ships by the Spaceport Manager. Once we understood the controls we each set off on an exploratory flight at relatively low hyper-velocity speeds. This enabled us to gain some familiarity with the systems and to return if any problems showed up. In most cases everybody was happy with the ships and after three or four weeks testing, we returned to base for a final briefing by the Superior. He again emphasised the importance of this mission for the future of our planet. In essence he said that if we can find intelligent creatures in other parts of the universe they might give us a reason for our existence and the purpose of life. Wow, high-level stuff! As a new young ätman I thought to myself it's great that I am considered important; although at that time I didn't really appreciate the full significance of the project.

We were given instructions to go to the main energy supply room in the Spaceport to plug ourselves in for a full day of supercharging before our departure. Then after good wishes and handshaking all round, we each went off to our spaceships and within minutes had them in the air in a long queue, levitated by the reaction between the dark matter and the surface of our planet. I then slowly increased the dark matter reaction till my ship reached the speed of Mach 5 (5 times the speed of sound) and switched on the scramjet system to achieve Mach 15 while still within the planet's atmosphere. Next I fired a ballistic rocket for injection out of planetary orbit and towards Proxima Centauri, our wonderful star. Within moments I left the atmosphere travelling on a parabolic orbit towards Proxima Centauri and further increased speed by electron injection. Next I zoomed in close to Proxima so that its gravitational pull further increased the ship's speed. Finally I activated the dark energy module and warped into a gravity wave that carried me out into space at very close to the speed of light.

Having got my ship into a flight path matching the curvature of the universe, I lay down on the bed and switched all my systems off with the alarm set to wake me every year. When I awoke I quickly checked all systems and made sure that there had been no signals indicating an intelligent species. Then I lay down and switched off for another year. I continued this pattern and during the 4th year there was a very small signal on the biological animal recorder. While there was no cognition response it did seem worth investigating; so I adjusted the warp path towards the source of the signal.

After a short time it was clear that I was heading towards a star with quite a few planets around it – something like eight or nine. From a distance it appeared that only one of these planets was the source of the biological signal. I decided that this particular solar system was worth investigating and activated the dark energy module to reduce warp speed. At the lower speed it took just over six months to reach the outskirts of the solar system and I travelled in towards the nuclear powered star at its centre. Most of the planets seemed lifeless rocky entities, although one had four moons; one of which had some indication of elementary biological life. The most interesting planet was largely blue in colour and had a strong biological signal. So I made a direct approach to this one. Steadily slowing my speed and adjusting trajectory, I went into orbit around the planet at a height of 900 kilocubits (just over 400 km).

I studied the planet with all the technological equipment mounted in the spaceship. From my observations over several months I discovered that there were many similarities to our own planet, with a few relatively minor differences. The planet took 365.25 of its days to circle around the star at the centre of its solar system – i.e. a year. Of course our planet has 361.4 days in a year. To avoid confusion in this presentation I will use earth years, which is how I measured time while I was on Earth. Also, I should explain that when I speak of time before now, I will use Earth years before 2020 – the year that I left that planet. Later I will explain the strange calendar system of earth people. You should also realise that it is now 5 years since I left Earth, because I had to travel the 4.24 light years distance from Earth to Ragnarök.

From rates of radioactive decay, I estimated the age of this planet and its solar system as approximately 4.54 billion years, which compares to our planet's 4.81 billion years. Thus we have had some 270 million extra years for our development and evolution. It occurred to me that the planet I was visiting might well evolve as we have. I will say more about that after I have described the two remarkably interesting, but very different, evolutions of living matter on the one planet that I had the great fortune to observe.

With the optical detector I saw a great collection of large biological animals moving around the dry land areas of the planet and also large swimming species in the watery regions, which covered much of the planet. The land animals appeared to be scaly, something like our crocodiles. The remote audio detector picked up loud sounds made by the animals. Most of these sounds did not contain much in the way of intelligent message communication although occasionally some calls were repeated and I noticed that when this happened, all the nearby animal species took fright and ran into hiding. After observing for a while I noted that some species consumed bushes and plants, much like our animals on Ragnarök, but other species attacked these animals in a most dreadful way and ate them by chewing and swallowing through the mouth.

This consumption of one animal species by another reminded me of the stories I had heard about animals on our own planet many millions of years ago, before they were educated by the psychologically trained ätmans. The process that was happening on the planet below me was so disgusting that I decided I should go down and see if I could educate the meat-eating creatures.

Using the dark energy module I slowed my speed to ensure an entry into the planetary atmosphere with very little air-friction that could cause excessive heating. Using the dark matter levitation I made a soft landing on a dry section of the planet not far from the large meat-eating creatures.

As soon as the spaceship was on the ground I activated the digging facility so that within a few seconds the whole ship was buried and out of sight. Then I pushed the escape tube to the surface for my exploration. Before leaving the spaceship I put on my invisibility cloak with its massive array of tiny television cameras and monitors, arranged so that when switched on, any observer is presented with the image of objects from the other side of the cloak. Thus it is completely transparent and hides anybody wearing it. Of course I had this switched off, but wore it in case any creatures became aggressive.

Chapter 5

The Distant Planet 250 million years ago.

I arose to the surface of the planet and found myself in a green wonderland. There were green leafy bushes growing everywhere and tall elegant trees with long limbs stretching into the sky, each covered in thick foliage. The surface itself was made up of fine particles and when I scratched a hole I found red squirmy worms. My chemical analyser showed that the atmosphere was just under 80% nitrogen and just over 20% oxygen with small amounts of other gases. Thus it would be a satisfactory place for the biological species on our own planet to live.

I could hear grunting and heavy breathing noises coming from behind a nearby bush. So I walked over to the bush and peering through the leaves I saw a beast standing on two legs with its head held high; two front arms or legs extending down from its chest. The head was relatively small and it opened its mouth very wide revealing large jagged teeth. Its length from head to toe was roughly 4 cubits (just under 2 m) when it lifted its head high it was about 3 cubits above the ground.

The animal walked forward with a jumping motion and came around the bush where I was standing. It bellowed loudly as soon as it saw me and came rushing towards me trying to claw at me with its front paws. I deflected the blows easily enough and made the same bellowing noise as it had uttered. This seemed to stop it for a moment or two and so I tried to pat it gently as we do with our animals. However this merely enraged it and it snapped at my hand, damaging my biological skin slightly. I thought there was a possibility that I might be badly damaged, so I switched on my invisibility cloak and moved away from the animal. It was clearly confused by this and looked around desperately.

I decided to follow the animal as it moved through the beautiful forest region. It moved quite fast and, maintaining my invisibility, I stayed 30 to 40 cubits behind it so it was unaware of my presence. After travelling some distance the creature stopped and crouched down, peering through a bush at some other animals quietly grazing in a grassy glen. Waiting till one of the grass-eating animals was close to the bush, the animal that I had been following leapt out and grabbed it round the neck. There was a loud squealing noise and then the victim fell to the ground, lifeless. The attacking animal proceeded to rip the carcass to pieces, which it swallowed. I was repulsed by this procedure, but without violence on my part I could not do anything to stop it. My software conscience sought to justify this by the reflection that I was a visitor on a strange planet and it was my role to observe, not to interfere.

For some months I wandered many kilocubits around my arrival point. I saw many curious biological species. There were small creatures that crawled on the surface or burrowed into the soil. Most of these had clean skin, but a few of the larger burrowers had a scaly outer layer. Many of the larger animals walked around mainly on their back legs since they had relatively short legs at the front. It seemed that the majority of these fed themselves by eating grass or leaves and about one third of them attacked and ate the grass-eaters. The largest of any I saw was 5 cubits (about 2.3 m) long and this creature stretched up to the leaves of a tree 4 cubits (just under 2 m) above the ground.

I saw many of the grass eating animals killed and eaten, leaving little residue. Occasionally I noted both grass-eaters and meat-eaters, as they got older became weak, fell down and the life-force left them. An empty body remained on the ground. Soon after death the squirmy wormy things came out of the soil to eat the flesh so that within a few days the internal bone structure of the creature was revealed. Often this was covered by drifting soils and turned into mud when rain fell. It was clear that all the creatures on this planet have a limited life cycle.

As with the biological animals on Ragnarök, there did not seem to be any provision for refurbishment of individual creatures. However new individuals were created by a method similar to the biological species on our planet. Periodically two members of the same species would approach each other. One of these would reveal a small protrusion and this was pressed into a cavity on the other animal. Apparently some fluid was transferred between the animals and when they separated it seemed that the one with the cavity was slightly chemically changed and over the coming weeks its body swelled. Although this procedure mirrored that of the larger animals on our planet, the result was different because, instead of producing a small animal through the cavity, the animals on this planet produced hard oval objects that sat on the ground for several more weeks. After a time the objects formed surface cracks that grew until the object fractured into two pieces and a new small animal appeared.

Remembering that biological species on our planet seem to benefit from a process of evolution which increased their physical structure and cognitive ability over successive generations, I decided to return to my spaceship and lie dormant for a few hundred years to see if the creatures of this planet also had an evolutionary syndrome.

Chapter 6

Evolution 250 million to 65 million Years Ago.

I was reenergised after being switched off for just under 100 million years and immediately made preparations to rise to the surface of the planet. On reaching the ground I found myself in a large open area where trees had been torn down and looking around I saw several gigantic animals that had caused this damage. They were similar in shape to creatures I had seen 100 million years before, but very much larger. Clearly there had been evolutionary changes. Some of the animals were about 55 cubits (25 m) long and they grabbed the leaves and boughs on trees some 40 cubits (18 m) high. Every so often they would pull a complete tree down and the smaller members of the species would greedily eat the leaves on the fallen tree. I had not activated my invisibility cloak, but the animals took little notice of me as I walked around.

Suddenly the whole group started bellowing and looking around anxiously. A somewhat smaller creature with a very large head and a wide-open mouth showing vicious teeth came running into the clearing on its back legs, balancing itself with its long tail. It charged up to one of the smaller animals eating leaves of the fallen tree and with one mighty crunch it bit into the neck of the animal and then proceeded to tear and swallow the skin, flesh and bone. By the time it had finished, all the other tree-eating animals had moved out of sight. The meat-eater spotted me and charged towards me with a great bellowing noise. I very quickly switched on my invisibility cloak and stepped out of its path.

Then I observed another creature. Its forelegs extended out from its body and a thin skin-like material stretched back towards the tail. This enabled it to use the atmosphere for aerodynamic flight and indeed, as soon as I moved towards it, a flutter of its forelegs launched it into the air. It glided smoothly over the length of the clearing and landed gently on a tree. The meat-eating creature ran towards it and tried to jump in the air, but the flyer was well above and in no danger.

I spent a year or two observing the various creatures and noted that, while they were sentient beings, they did not have sophisticated communication skills. There appeared to be respect and support for individuals of the same species, but quite marked aggression to other creatures. Aggression was very obvious between meat eaters and vegetable eaters – to be expected since the vegetable eaters preferred not to be eaten!

I returned to the spaceship and continued to rise every million years, but did not find any technological developments, nor was there any apparent interest in considering the reason for life or why their planet might exist. Hence 65 million years ago I decided there was little to learn by staying on this remote part of the universe. The flora and the water regions were beautiful and the biosphere was just right for carbon-based creatures, but there was little we could learn from their way of life. Evolution was taking place, but it was very slow and did not seem to be throwing up high-level cognition in any of the creatures.

After fully recharging in the spaceship I switched on the dark matter ejection to lift above the surface and then increased the dark matter energy to attain orbit around the planet. I was about to set the controls to achieve hypervelocity and hence return to Ragnarök, when the emergency object-detector alarm reported the approach of a large rocky asteroid on a collision course towards the planet below me. This seemed to offer an opportunity to gain information about the mechanics of colliding astrological bodies and so I decided to remain above the planet at a height where I should be safe. I went into orbit at 900 kilocubits above the surface.

The massive asteroid went past my ship travelling about a thousand times less than lightspeed. I experienced quite severe rocking from the gravitational pull as it went past. Then it tangentially entered planetary atmosphere creating a spectacular fiery display of sparks for a few minutes before slamming into a desert region on the surface of the planet. There was a brilliant flash of white light indicating a very high collision temperature. Within milliseconds a great cloud of dust and smoke arose from the point of impact and with the remaining momentum of the asteroid, particles of dust rapidly spread around the biosphere so that in about 24 hours the whole planet was hidden from my view by the dark layer of dust and ash that now comprised most of the atmosphere.

For several weeks I could not visually see the surface of the planet. My detectors showed the major features of the surface remained, while the globe itself had changed its trajectory and reduced its rotational speed slightly. The biological detectors dropped rapidly towards zero in the first week and then stabilised at a very low number indicating that most life had ceased, but a small amount remained.

I continued in my orbit and after some three years the dust cloud surrounding the planet seemed to settle or disburse into the atmosphere so that I re-established visual contact. Then I decided to return to the surface in the same manner as before; burying the spaceship about five cubits below the surface. When I arose to the surface I found a thick layer of ash lying everywhere and many large trees collapsed on the ground from the weight of ash. At first I could not see any moving biological species, but then I noticed small lizards and insects crawling around and I saw two small flying creatures. In some cases feathers were growing on the skin of these flyers. Digging into the ground I discovered quite large numbers of the red worms that appeared to have survived the asteroid impact satisfactorily.

This presented an interesting experimental situation. Here was a planet with minimal biological lifeforms:

> Could survivors of the catastrophic event regenerate the abundant life that had existed before the collision?

> Would the large scaly creatures with long back legs and short front legs be re-established?

> Or could evolution take another path?

I decided this chance opportunity justified my remaining on Earth. So I returned to the ship and switched myself off for 40 million years, as that seemed an appropriate time for any significant evolution to have occurred.

Chapter 7

Life after the Asteroid Disaster till 25 million years ago

I rose to the surface not expecting much change, but I was very surprised to find a completely different land to the one I had seen 40 million years previously. Everywhere tall trees had grown, the grass was clean and green and I even saw coloured flowers. While I was standing and looking around a large furry creature broke through a bush not far away. It was something like a bear; walking on its four equal-sized legs, but unlike a bear it had a very long snout and it was using this to scoop up ants that it swallowed in large numbers. The animal took little notice of me. It simply walked past with a low grunting noise and moved off busily sucking up ants.

Using antimatter to levitate I travelled over most of the planet observing quite a wide array of biological species most of them covered in thick layers of fur. I was particularly struck by several groups of animals that had a likeness to our own primates, in that they frequently walked upright on their back legs and used their front legs or arms for various tasks such as scratching each other, climbing trees and even holding little sticks to get honey out of cavities in trees. These primates had developed a wide range of noises, which they used as basic communication; such as telling others that some danger was approaching. There were different groups living together. The members of particular groups having different colours from light grey to dark brown and in various sizes from roughly 1 cubit up to 3 cubits (½ to 1½ meters) high.

In the sky I saw many flying creatures flapping their forelimbs and these were all thickly covered with feathers. They were masters of aerodynamic flight; zooming effortlessly between the branches of trees and uttering musical notes that seemed to be some sort of communication between different individuals. I tried to interpret this with my language translator, but did not get any very precise message. They appeared to be expressing an emotion of joy or happiness and asking other members to share that emotion with them. This concept of emotion is apparently something that our species is lacking and hence it seemed an important part of my mission to study this before returning. Clearly the bird creatures were the most advanced members of the planet and I expected that if they continued evolving as they had so far, they could well reach sophisticated cognition, which may provide a useful model to develop improved emotional software for our species.

The rate of evolution that had occurred in the past 40 million years surprised me. Evolution, which had modified and advanced the previous creatures, was clearly operating much more rapidly and producing very different species since the asteroid collision. I was certainly interested in observing and recording these changes so I captured many hologram images of every animal that I saw and am happy to display these to the Planetary Council members now.

The Council chamber darkened slightly and many biological creatures appeared and started moving amongst all the council members who were able to look at them closely as they went past, even though they were simply technological images. The Council Chamber broke into uproar as members started asking many questions –

Were these animals noisy?
Were they aggressive?
Did they eat each other?
Did they die when they got older?
How did they create new members of the species?

Horatio went on to explain that the animals were much like those currently on Ragnarök. He agreed that they certainly died or were killed and to maintain numbers they used the method that council members would be familiar with on their own planet. A protrusion on one animal was inserted into another animal and, in due course, that other animal produced a living offspring. In most cases a new animal appeared as a small edition of the parent animals, although in some cases an egg was emitted and this broke open after a time to reveal a new small animal – birds in particular, favoured this process.

Returning to my spaceship I decided to switch myself off for only 15 million years, as the rate of evolution seemed quite rapid. Indeed, on next rising to the surface I found considerable change. There were quite a few larger creatures, including some leather skinned creatures larger than our elephants and they had very long white tusks. The birds had evolved into a variety of different species in a whole collection of wonderful colours, but their communication, although rather shrill and pleasant, was still quite primitive. The cognitive development I had anticipated for the species had not occurred. On the other hand there were some groups of primates that were sounding quite interesting and behaving in a way that suggested real cognition and emotional interaction between individuals with hugging and stroking. This group was worth further study.

After a further 5 million year resting in my spaceship I rose to find evolution had developed vast arrays of new species on land and also in surrounding waters. I took particular note of the primates. I observed a group, who had rather less fur than others and walked more or less upright on their two back legs. They were becoming quite dexterous with their articulated front paws; similar to our hands. They lived in a fairly isolated region, which they later called Africa. I decided this group might be worth studying in future years.

It was interesting to note how the process of evolution seemed to ensure that creatures in different regions developed various characteristics to suit the climate and environment where they lived. As ätmans we have only developed by correctly designed software and mechanical structures, but this biological life evolved and changed automatically depending on conditions.

The rate of change of biological life on this planet made it clear to me that I should return to the surface for further study fairly soon, so I switched myself off for only 3 million years before rising again.

On my return – 2 million years ago – I immediately went to the region where the primates with little hair existed. There were big changes. All the animals stood more or less upright and walked or ran with a positive gait. They gathered food by scratching up insects, picking plants and seeds and occasionally they grabbed and killed small animals. They collected in different tribes and I noticed that there was often some animosity between tribes resulting in physical attack. They clearly gained great pleasure from tightly holding or hugging each other. Their vocal chords were more flexible than most other animals so they were able to communicate a relatively wide range of messages from one to the other.

Other animals, including other primates found in many of the tropical parts of the planet, had evolved to some extent, but not nearly as fast as the hairless primates. There had been some movement of the landmasses so that continents had changed shape and moved to different climatic regions on the planet. This had influenced the evolution of some of the species.

However the land movements were relatively slow and species had often migrated in a reverse direction to that of the land, so they maintained a suitable climatic temperature for themselves.

The rapid changes in the hairless primates were really interesting. I felt, if I returned in just one million years I might find significant developments.

Chapter 8

Evolution of the Primates – 1 million years ago.

I returned to the surface just 1 million years ago. The development of the hairless primates was quite noticeable. They were standing straight and walking very confidently. There were differing types, some with very heavy protruding foreheads and strong jaws, others fine boned, very fast runners and graceful in their movements. All of them had established significant verbal communication using a wide range of grunts and whistles produced with the throat and lips.

The rapid and extensive evolution of these primates was indeed very interesting to me and so I reduced my 'switch-off-times' underground in the spaceship to a mere 10,000 years and repeated this a few times so that I could study the detailed changes in these animals. On my second return – some 800,000 years ago – the primate species had learnt the technology for creating fire. They used this for cooking, for warmth and as a defence against attacking animals. They had also learned how to shape animal skins so these could be wrapped around their bodies when the temperature was low. There were still not many of these primates – less than a quarter million – and they remained in one relatively small geographic area in part of the region later called Africa. They were clearly afraid of and dominated by most other animals, although they did attack and kill smaller creatures for food.

As I continued my observations each 10,000 years I saw a slow growth in the population of the hairless primates. I also noted a general increase in the size of the head relative to the rest of the body and on several occasions I watched the emergence of a new animal from the body of its mother. Clearly the larger head made it more difficult for the new creature to emerge and from the noise emitted by the mother it appeared this may have caused some pain. It was also interesting that newly created primates had very few of the skills required to survive by themselves, so that their tribes looked after their bodily needs and protected them from other animals. Most other new young animal species were instantly capable of running and looking after themselves immediately after birth, but not these hairless primates.

When I looked again 300,000 years ago I carefully examined the different sub-species of the hairless, upright, primates. I noted that there were six separate sub-species. They were all rather aggressive to each other. The fine-boned subset appeared the most aggressive; dominating the others by their superior communication and cooperation skills. Employing antimatter levitation I rose to some 2000 cubits (about 900 m) and travelled over the region where these particular primates lived. I counted a total population of about three quarters of a million.

I continued my cyclical switch-on and switch-off observations of the developing primates. In each 10,000 year period there was not great change, just a steady increase in numbers and developing communication and basic technological skills for harvesting grasses and seeds and capturing and killing small animals for food. 150,000 years ago I did another count from above and found there were nearly 1 million of these semi-advanced primates.

Chapter 9

Migration from Africa – 80,000 years ago

As the years went by, the population of sophisticated primate animals grew rapidly; largely based on a good supply of food, shelter from the elements, ability to defend themselves against attack from other animals and some skill in assisting each other when illnesses struck. By 80,000 years ago, the overcrowding and degradation of the soil with little crop rotation and rising salt, together with chaotic behaviour by many of the group leaders, encouraged adventurous members of the more intelligent species to start a migration to other regions.

To a large extent the animals journeyed simply by walking on their own 2 feet, but in addition they had devised primitive vessels to float on the seas – some of these driven by wind, others by paddling. In a period of some 2,000 years the migrating animals had made their way all over the lands they called Africa, the Middle East, Europe, Asia and, by a series of island hops, to distant Australia.

I travelled to various places on the planet using my levitation. I switched on my invisibility cloak and mixed freely with the animals. Using my translating module I listened to the conversations between individuals. Their cognition was growing rapidly and they extended their discussions well beyond immediate pragmatic situations.

Many strange ideas were formed by these creatures; one that has been maintained right up till the time I left the planet is that they are fundamentally different from all the other animals. Indeed as their language grew, they formed a belief that they were not mere animals, but creations of some supernatural being. They started to call themselves 'humans', 'people' or Homo sapiens ('the wise ones'). In support of the belief in their difference, indeed superiority, they endeavoured to hide their animal attributes by wrapping themselves in clothes and hiding away from the rest of the tribe when engaging in any animal functions such as defecating, or engrossed in the special close embrace that started the creation of offspring.

To avoid confusion in my narrative I will now distinguish these particular primate animals from other animals by using the names they adopted: 'humans' for the species, 'person' for an individual creature and 'people' for a collection of advanced primate animals.

I made quick inspection trips around the planet every thousand years or so and noted how the various groups developed. One striking feature was the change in skin pigmentation. 80,000 years ago all the hairless primates had a dusky complexion – brown verging on black skin colour. As time went by, the primates living in the northern regions of the planet seemed to have some degeneration of their skin pigment, so they became progressively lighter in appearance. This was most probably influenced by reduced sunlight hours, although biological genetic changes may also have had an effect.

The group that travelled to Australia, as it eventually became known, found themselves isolated as intercontinental movements created a large land mass surrounded by ocean. A reasonably large number of people had reached this area 65,000 years ago. They spread out across the big island, establishing separate tribal entities, each with their own slightly different customs and practices. The land was somewhat barren relative to other parts of the planet, but these people were careful in studying the climate and natural resources, so they were able to live comfortably in small groups. Usually their lifestyle was relatively relaxed. They found sufficient vegetable food without too much difficulty and they showed considerable inventiveness in making weapons for capturing animals, which they ate. All the groups had access to fire, so they could cook meals; keep themselves warm and periodically burn areas of scrubland to reduce the risk of uncontrolled bushfires and enhance the growth of food plants for future years.

The Australian people – although they didn't call themselves that– retained a healthy brown skin colour; varying in different regions of their island. 50,000 years ago their community arrangements were far more advanced than any people in the northern hemisphere. Although they were spread widely over their land they formed relatively small tribal groups with similar laws and cultures in all districts. Peace was maintained within groups by strong myths and legends, which prescribed acceptable behaviour for interaction between individuals. Strict punishments were specified for anyone disobeying the established customs. Occasionally there were conflicts between tribes, but these were rare – usually arising if the imaginary border between tribes was crossed by individuals from another tribe. The tribal borders were sometimes delineated by physical features such as rivers or hills, but usually they were purely imaginary concepts accepted by the neighbouring tribes.

Using my translating machine I discovered there were some 400 different languages in Australia. Apart from their constant discussion about food, climate and story/gossip concerning relationships between men and women, people were beginning to consider major philosophical topics such as:

How had the earth been created?
How had individual features, such as hills and rivers formed?
How had life been established?
Was there a Creator?
Was there a purpose to living?
Could they bring rain or improve the environment by ritualistic dancing or singing?

They demonstrated wonderful imagination and ingenious thinking. Many of the tribal groups, independently, spoke of an illusory 'dream time' when the earth had formed and they invented stories to explain the formation of local geographic features, such as hills, rivers, etc. Often in their dancing and singing they truly believed that the dancer or singer embodied the real essence of any creature or earthly feature that they represented for the purpose of the ritual.

The tribal groups in the Australian continent maintained their well-ordered and comfortable existence until shortly before I left the planet. Unfortunately for them, in 1788 their lifestyle was turned upside down, by the arrival of pale skin people from the northern hemisphere equipped with technologically advanced weapons, diseases previously unknown on this land and a coordinated drive to acquire the whole continent. These new arrivals slowly overcame the inhabitants by conquering one tribe after another. The lack of coordination between the established tribes was a factor in the resistance against the newcomers. However they did put up a brave defence that went on for many years in different parts of the large island. Finally they were forced to accept integration with the foreigners.

Chapter 10

Northern Regions of the Planet – 10,000 years ago.

Changes came slowly in the northern regions of the globe. 80,000 years ago I had seen that the human animals lived in small family groups with frequent fighting between the groups and, because of lack of cooperation between individuals, there was considerable loss of human life from attacks by other animals The number of sub-species declined until only two major groups remained when I emerged to the surface 10,000 years ago. By that time a variety of weapons had been fashioned from sticks and stones, so that human animals were becoming dominant over other species.

I noticed some of the primates started to collect bundles of seeds and instead of eating these, planted them into the ground in orderly plots. In the following years they had very large quantities of seeds and did not need to travel far and wide to collect a crop. So they built themselves shelters and lived close to the fields they had formed. Also at about this time some humans piled stones to make walled, rectangular, spaces leaving a small gap through which they drove other animals and closed the gap with tree boughs to create a confinement zone. In this way they were able to periodically select a confined animal to kill for eating. Furthermore some of the imprisoned mammalian animals expressed milk intended for feeding their newborn young, but the innovative primates removed the young animals and extracted milk for themselves.

These changes, about 9,000 years ago, later known as the agricultural revolution brought major changes to the way of life of these primates. Living in the one location and with their now relatively advanced communication skills they specialised in separate tasks – some members of the group spent most of the day out amongst the crops tending the food plants; others looked after the farmed animals; milking them and ensuring they were fattened for food; while others specialised in building dwellings and fences.

These largely hairless primates had been clothing themselves with skins for a few thousand years, but now they started to create cloth by weaving various plant materials together. They fashioned quite elaborate clothing, some brightly coloured by soaking in water mixed with coloured plants or finely crushed coloured stones

All this new activity involved considerable reorganisation. Where people had previously lived a very casual life; wandering about to collect food and storing very little, they now found themselves needing to work long periods of time at their specialised tasks.

Hunter gatherers had enjoyed plenty of time for gossiping and storytelling, which humans love to do. Now for most people there were just a few moments for relaxation after a tiring day of work. In this restructuring a few dominant individuals took a controlling role, managing the activities and telling others what tasks they should perform. In many cases the dominant animals claimed to have special powers conferred upon them by some mysterious unseen force or supernatural beings. These dominant people (that were called 'leaders') set up a comfortable lifestyle for themselves with plenty of time for recreation and discussions, which they called 'meetings'. They made rules about how all the others should behave, even to the extent of deciding how much of the harvested food should be allocated to each individual and how much time must be spent on allotted tasks. Any person not having a 'job' (a task allocated by the leader) was regarded very poorly and often not given any of the shared tribal food or comforts.

The people living near the river they called the Nile found that seeds planted in this region yielded outstandingly productive crops. This encouraged more people to move there and 6500 years ago they formed themselves into a close-living commune. They gave it the name Sumer and they were known as Sumerians – citizens of the world's first nation with several separate urban centres.

The Sumerian way of life was later called civilisation and eventually adopted by groups all over the planet;

although there were significant differences in the rules or laws that were established in different places. As I moved over the planet I noted the rise of cities in the lands they called Egypt, India, China and, somewhat later, the northern land mass which became known as Europe.

During the period 8,000 till about 6,000 years ago, the humans demonstrated wonderful imagination and creative thought. They seemed unaware of the evolution process and, as I have mentioned, many of them became convinced that they had been put onto their planet by some mysterious supernatural process implemented by an imaginary all-powerful being. They considered themselves stewards or guardians of all other animals. This classic claim was clearly ridiculous since they treated other animals very badly and drove many species to extinction. The animals they used for meat or milk were imprisoned in walled fields and newborns were removed from their mothers to provide a milk supply for humans.

As the migration across the planet continued, the creation stories were modified and changed, but mostly people believed they had some sort of internal kernel, often called a soul or a spirit, which in some inexplicable fashion continued to exist after their physical body had lost its biological life.

If they contemplated it at all, most humans saw the earth as a massive flat plane living in space. Some people thought the flat plane might be held up by huge animals, possibly elephants or turtles. Some imaginative stories suggested oversize humans held the earth on their shoulders – Atlas and Hercules were names suggested for these giants. However most people accepted that the ground they walked on was flat, that the sun rose in the east each morning, that the moon and stars brightened the night sky, that they would find sufficient food to eat and that they could shelter in naturally formed caves or make protective huts from boughs of trees.

An increasing number of humans felt a need to have some convincing explanation for their existence and the existence of the planet. This need appears to be related to the evolution of their brains, or as we might say on our planet – the refinement of their software algorithms. This enabled deeper, reflective thought processes. In many regions there was a strengthening belief that some intelligent being or beings (which they called gods) must exist in some paranormal form. The simple concept that the universe and life itself might have developed by a series of random events did not seem credible to many people.

Verbal communication improved remarkably and many of the imaginative stories were handed on from generation to generation. However, the human brain stores information very imprecisely; thus stories changed regularly. Recognising the unreliability of human memory, marks on stone tablets and other medium were developed and codified to record events and stories. This invention, known as writing, was achieved at about the same time (5,000 years ago), in the Middle East, in China and in the central part of the American continent. For many years humans had scratched, cut or chipped markings on stone, which depicted physical things – such as people and other animals, but 5,000 years ago people started to draw symbols, which codified sounds, so that spoken words could be recorded. Thus stories, ideas and imaginary speculations could be passed down from generation to generation relatively accurately.

The extraordinary ingenuity of humans is illustrated in a story that was developed about two imaginary people, Adam and Eve, said to be the first humans on this planet. This story has varied from time to time, but usually the story goes that these two people lived in a wonderful world full of natural fruit trees. Clothing had not been invented, so just like all the other animals, they walked around naked. Some celestial entity instructed them how to behave and stressed that they should not eat the fruit from one particular tree. However a snakelike reptile spoke to Eve one day telling her to take and eat an apple from the tree. She took a bite and also gave one to Adam. Immediately both of them suffered some form of hallucination and felt embarrassed about being naked. They also suddenly believed themselves responsible for the planet and they should forego the simple, easy, forager life they were living and change to a life of drudgery and continual work. This quaint story is a good illustration of the astonishing imagination of Homo sapiens. The story formed a part of the writings by a group of men living in the land known as the Middle

East. Their writing became part of a standalone book known as Genesis. It was eventually incorporated into a tome known as the Bible regarded as rather important by many of the human species. I will elaborate on this later.

Chapter 11

Rise of Philosophy and Religion in the last 5,000 years

As I made my annual trips around the planet, stopping to use my invisibility cloak and my language translation device, I was able to closely follow development of ideas amongst widely separated humans. It became very clear that the thinking processes of these Homo sapiens all over the planet had evolved to a high level 2,600 to 2,000 years ago.

About 2,500 years ago in a region known as Greece several humans had arranged their lives so that they had time to meditate and discuss in great detail the nature of their existence and the way communities might be structured for the benefit of everyone. This group were mainly males of the species and they depended on female partners and other people they called slaves, to provide for all their bodily needs, so that they could claim a superior status and spend much of their time feeding on each other's ideas and expanding concepts passed down from one group to another, in both oral and written form. In this situation it seems that their cognitive capacity developed significantly so they contributed many new ideas about logical thinking and fundamental understanding of the physical world. They called these developments philosophy and natural philosophy (later known as science). These men built on each other's ideas for several generations over some 500 years to establish an ideas-database still accessed by human society.

One of the people who stood out amongst these Greeks was Socrates, who went into public spaces and gave long talks about the need to develop logical algorithms rather than using spiritual imagination to explain the nature of the universe and the management of human society. One of his students, Plato, took note of all these ideas and, with further contributions of his own, wrote them down for future generations. I was fortunate to meet Plato in Athens 2,395 years ago. I switched off my invisibility cloak and approached him in the room where he was writing. He was a bit shocked because he found my appearance completely foreign, but I assured him I was not a spiritual manifestation and that I fully accepted his logical explanation of the nature of things. With this established he was ready to talk with me even though he found it strange for life to exist on the stars in his sky. Indeed I suspect he thought I was not truthful in this matter.

Much of his thinking related to the importance of developing rules and procedures for peaceful coexistence amongst peoples. He was particularly concerned about just and unjust governors and the rewards that they sought as leaders. Although he was well informed about the history of his own region he had very little knowledge of the spread of Homo sapiens over the whole planet. By subtle questioning I realised he knew nothing of the well-advanced living arrangements of people in the far-off Southland of Australia and little of the developing civilisation in China. I was careful not to inform him about this, because it might have influenced his philosophical thinking. A major thrust of his ideas and those of his former teacher, Socrates, was the need to logically face reality and not be swayed by stories of unearthly spiritual realms.

Plato did not believe in the many stories of interaction of superhuman gods in the affairs of everyday life, as did many of his fellow Athenian citizens. Nor was he a believer in the concept of one Supreme Being monitoring people's minds and sitting on a day of judgement that led to heaven or hell after death, as had been proposed by Zoroaster in Persia about a thousand years before Plato was born. Plato also told me that he had heard stories written by the Israelites of Canaan who believed there was some mystical entity they called Yahweh who had created their planet, watched over them in life and controlled their life after death. Rather than supernatural ideas, Plato was much more concerned about logical thinking and justice between people; ideas that his mentor, Socrates, had died for. His driving concern was for equality with a strong, but wise central government, allowing people to grow in happiness. Ethical behaviour was his major interest and he outlined his understandings in numerous writings. I noted that many of his ideas were embedded in societies that were established around the world, millennia later.

In many regions the period 3,000 years ago till about 2,000 years ago was important for the human species in their exploration for a meaning to life and for organising society in large groups. At the middle of this period I spent some time in China listening to a widely respected man, Confucius. He espoused the need for a strong family, with ethics based on mutual respect and the development of morals within each individual, which provide skilled judgements rather than rigid community rules. His ideas strongly supporting human rights – although ignored in many succeeding human organisations – have remained firm and indeed were written into a global body called the "United Nations" just over 70 years ago.

About the same time that Confucius was presenting his ideas in China, I heard of a wise man in India who was teaching about life and ways of living. His name was Siddhattha Gotama, but he was widely known as Buddha. Like Confucius he believed in avoiding suffering for all the human species, but he went further and aimed to avoid suffering for all sentient beings, which he defined as all entities with consciousness. Listening to his talks I realised that many of his ideas need to be considered by our species. We ätmans are not biologically living creatures, yet our software enables us to analyse situations and reach decisions to take actions that we may consider necessary. Does this mean that we have consciousness? Are we in fact sentient beings? I pondered these matters for several days whist following Buddha as he walked from place to place in India giving talks. I joined his audience on many occasions, but retained my invisibility cloak so that nobody knew I was there. I formed the view that the ideas of Buddha should help us in considering future life on our own planet. I will summarise my thoughts towards the end of the presentation when I will give some conclusions and recommendations.

There was so much discussion and thinking going on around the planet at this time I did not go back to the spaceship for a rest, but just made quick stops to revitalise my body. The Middle East area of the planet seemed to be a region of very active thinkers. The Israelites of Canaan wrote the history of their tribe on parchment that was often stored in clay pots in the dry area of the land around a very low lying inland sea known as the "Dead Sea". They had a strong belief in a spiritual Being who listens to their thoughts and makes judgements about their behaviour. There were different cultural groups – some who established very strict observance to the rules or laws; others who thought it more important to love and respect the Superior Being and to love and support one another.

Just over 2,000 years ago a Jewish carpenter called Jesus embraced the ideas of love similar to those in the Dead Sea Scrolls. He proposed a simple lifestyle without any strict religious practices. Jesus formed a small group that travelled around the district now known as Israel, preaching this message. The powerful rule-based Jewish groups felt their authority threatened and they arranged for Jesus to be killed by the Roman occupiers of the country.

I took little interest in this Jewish group led by Jesus because they were a very small band and it seemed unlikely that their ideas would have much impact beyond the local community. In this I was proved wrong when some 70 years later four scribes wrote remarkable stories about Jesus; alleging that he arose and walked amongst his people three days after he had been executed.

In fact the stories about the life and teaching of Jesus attracted considerable interest and many people, long after his death, asserted that he had special powers bestowed upon him by a mysterious God. Roman leaders, who controlled most of this region, saw growing numbers of Jesus-followers as a threat to social order and so they brutally and publicly repressed them. Remarkably this seemed to encourage a growth in the number of followers, who now called themselves Christians, or followers of Christ.

In the next 300 years the Roman Empire became embroiled in political disputes and the Emperor, Constance, under threat from rivals, set up his headquarters in a new city, Constantinople, in the land of Turkey. Noting the remarkable success of the people calling themselves Christians and also influenced by the views of his mother, he proclaimed Christianity the official religion for Rome. This ensured a rapid growth in followers that has continued for two millennia. Now 2.3 billion people or 31% of the global population declare themselves to be Christians – a remarkable result from the initial group of ten!

Chapter 12

The Northern Hemisphere–
human years: 0 to 600

People started to keep track of the years by making calendars, initially carved in stone. There were different starting points, but about some 600 years ago a calendar was proposed, based on the year that was estimated as the time of the birth of Jesus. Surprisingly nearly all the people on the planet, even those who did not accept Jesus as any special sort of person, adopted this calendar. So to simplify my explanation, I will now use this calendar as I explain the events in the last two millennia.

I mentioned earlier that in year 313 the Roman Emperor Constantine decreed that belief in Jesus having a special relationship to the paranormal God of the Jews must be accepted by the Romans. This action ensured a continuing belief in the idea of a mystical creator and a mysterious consciousness after bodily death.

We, ätmans might consider life after death somewhat analogous to the wireless transfer of all our digital software that occurs with our refurbished into a new body. However the humans have developed an additional idea that on the demise of their physical body, their software, or consciousness, is transferred to some non-physical entity existing in a non-material space. There are different ideas about the details of this non-material existence, but it is a wildly held belief. Some people believe the non-material space is well above the earth, others think it is on the earth's surface as an invisible, undetectable envelope in which spirits reside. Presumably people want to go on living for ever, so they readily accept some form of continuing thought process, or after-life, even though there is no evidence of this.

In the year 610 an Arabian man, Mohammed, who had been born in the city of Mecca, after secluding himself periodically for several nights of prayer in a mountain cave, started to preach that he was a prophet sent by the same paranormal God who had sent Adam, Abraham, Moses, Jesus and other prophets to planet Earth. Mohammed claimed that an angel Gabriel had come to him in some spiritual or ethereal form to tell him of his status and to give him many instructions about how people should live on the planet. He wrote these things in a book that became known as the Koran or Quran. At that time Mecca was well known as a city whose people worshipped idols. One special idol was a large black stone known as the Kaaba – it had attracted pilgrimages from all over Arabia for many centuries before Mohammed's time. Mohammed spoke out against this idolatry and taught of One True God. This annoyed the local people who made a plan to kill him, but he escaped by moving to the nearby town of Medina.

I heard of Mohammed's teachings while I was travelling in a distant part of the desert. It sounded an interesting philosophy and so I made my way to Medina, where covered by my invisibility cloak, I was able to listen to and observe Mohammed and those listening to him. Clearly he was very dedicated to his belief and he was able to convince leaders and the good people of Medina that his message had validity. Mohammed was certainly an innovative thinker and so he, together with his rich and powerful friend, Abu Bekr, incorporated the black stone of Mecca as a holy monument within Islam, so that the pilgrimages to Mecca would continue and indeed grow. By this move the Islamic religion, with its definitive monotheism; simple faith in the rule and fatherhood of God and freedom from the past theologies, became the dominant faith throughout Arabia. The Kaaba stone was built into a larger black structure and has become the central feature of Islam, requiring disciples all over the world to face towards it as they say their prayers.

The wide acceptance of the teachings of Mohammed provided a strong base for the establishment of an Empire of Islam. Abu Bekr became leader after Mohammed's death in year 632. He was a strong character with good organisational skills and he set out to make the whole world Islamic. Military groups were established and in short order Syria, Damascus, Palmyra, Antioch and Jerusalem became strongholds of the Faith. Abu Bekr died two years later, but he had started the expansion policy and by 637, after a massive three day battle against a force using elephants, which I watched with great interest, most of Persia became part of the Muslim empire. Expansion continued across Turkestan until it reached the border of China, along the north coast of Africa to the Straits of Gibraltar and Spain and by 732 had reached the centre of France. Having occupied Egypt the Muslims now had a fleet of boats and they tried to occupy Constantinople, but were repelled.

Chapter 13

The Dark Ages in Europe – human years: 500 to 1500

With the expansion of the Muslim empire the influence of the European peoples had greatly diminished. People in the far north (known as the Nordic people) were still active and vital, but lived in a very restricted land mass. The Christian church with its centre at Rome was still quite active and kept the Latin language alive, with priests scattered all over Europe. There was great turmoil in the leadership of this church because they often appointed old men to the position they called the Pope, with the result that they died soon after taking up their position. To add to the confusion within the church, there was conflict with the Emperor in Constantinople, who did not accept the Pope in Rome as the successor to St Peter, the chief disciple of Jesus.

Throughout Europe there was no harmonized leadership. In most places small groups existed in a feudal economy with local leaders (usually men) and local rules or laws controlling the population – often harshly. At regular intervals the Nordic people raided parts of Europe killing and plundering as they went through the land. In addition, every few years a warlike group living to the north-west of Europe crossed the Alps to Northern Italy and proceeded to burn, rob and destroy established communities. This group became known as the Huns.

My emotional software – although limited – found the behaviour of these groups in Europe at this time, rightly known as the Dark Ages, quite disgusting and demoralising. However I was mildly encouraged when I met a man called Peter the Hermit who walked around in bare feet wearing primitive clothing and carrying a large wooden cross. He gathered crowds of people in the streets and preached a simple form of belief in the teachings of Jesus (who had become known as the Christ or Messiah) based on love between people. A great wave of enthusiasm was created and a group of ordinary people from Western Europe rose up in an uncoordinated fashion to charge on Jerusalem with the intention of reclaiming that city from the Muslims. This was known as the first Crusade. It reached Constantinople, but without leadership or effective strategy, it was overcome by the Turks who massacred most of the crusaders. A year later another crusade was launched under the leadership of the more disciplined Normans; they succeeded in occupying Jerusalem where they, in turn, brutally slaughtered men women and children in a horrifying blood bath. This really confused me, since they claimed to bring a message of universal love!

Although Christianity had now been embraced by many of the ordinary people in Europe, the rulers, including the Popes in Rome, did not seem to understand that religion depended on wide acceptance by the population. Instead, the Popes fought amongst themselves and a split developed between Christianity in Rome and in Greece. Fighting and wars became the way of life for over 300 years.

I found the situation in Europe unpleasant to watch and so I moved off to China where there were great developments in technology and organisation of their society. A group in the north of China known as the Mongols had established themselves as the dominant tribe, with excellent planning and management of their campaigns. In the year 1214 I accompanied Genghis Khan the leader of the Mongol Confederate as he occupied all of China and conquered India down to Lahore and much of South Russia. His people worshipped him so that he was recognised as the undisputed leader of a vast empire, but it is distressing to note that like many humans there were two sides to his personality and he is largely remembered for the brutal massacre of large numbers of civilians in the captured territories. His son Ogedei Khan succeeded him as leader and he continued the march to the west rapidly overrunning Poland and Hungary. I noted how the Khan dynasty had established rigid discipline amongst their troops and that they had the advantage of gunpowder used in field guns, which they developed. Perhaps more than all of this their Army leaders demonstrated brilliance in gathering intelligence about their enemies and meticulously timing their attacks.

Chapter 14

Remarkable Awakening of the Europeans

The Dark Ages of Europe continued for hundreds of years, dominated by the demands of the church for people to totally believe in the writings of the Bible put together by ancient people and interpreted by the Pope and priests to suit their own extravagant desires. In addition to the mantra, "believe what I say because I say it", the ordinary people were also periodically called upon to make war on other groups, as I have mentioned.

Things started to change slowly. Universities were established at Bologna, Paris, Oxford and other places in Europe by the 12th century. These studies and teachings were largely based on established dogma and law, but by the 13th century there were early stirrings as a few open minded scholars questioned the church leadership and increasingly studied philosophy and its component, natural philosophy. This period became known as the Renaissance (or 'rebirth') as people all over Europe started to re-examine and revive the remarkable knowledge and understanding of the ancient Arabs, Greeks and Romans.

The enthusiastic drive that characterised the three centuries of the Renaissance (roughly early 14th till the 16th century) seemed to start from the input of finances provided by the Medici family, who owned an Italian bank and a supported several very talented people. Two polymaths, with a wide range of interests and abilities, were Leonardo da Vinci and Michelangelo. Their artistic work together with their scientific and technological contributions set a pattern for many future generations. This period also saw elegant architectural construction in several European countries; much of it inspired from ancient times.

I heard about a man, Roger Bacon, at Oxford University who wrote long dissertations against the ignorance of human beings and the stupidity of hanging on to childish ideas just because they had been passed down from a few hundred or even thousands of years earlier. I was able to visit him and to hear some of the remarkably prescient ideas that he discussed with his friends. I was very careful to maintain my invisibility and not to make any remarks that might have influenced his thoughts. I was told by one of his friends that he once angrily remarked something along the lines – if we can overcome the ignorant dogma of men it may be possible to create machines for navigating without rowers, so that great ships suited to river or ocean, guided by one man, may be carried with greater speed than if they were full of men; likewise carts may be made without a draft animal and flying machines created. He had many ideas not accepted by his lords and masters, or indeed most of his peers. Much of his thinking was based on the idea that people should observe natural events with an unbiased eye and formulate explanations that satisfied the observations – irrespective of what ancient thinkers in their ignorance may have claimed. Because his ideas threatened the ruling authorities he was punished and jailed in an attempt to silence him. I was disappointed to see that human beings are so narrow-minded in their thinking that they cannot accept new observations and explanations. In later times Roger Bacon's approach was accepted and formed the basis of "scientific method" by subsequent generations.

After resting awhile and recreating my body in the spacecraft I returned to the surface and moved around various parts of Europe at the end of the 13th century. One big change I noticed was that the Homo sapiens had developed a procedure for rapidly printing the characters they used for communication, so that they produced many low-cost books. They were obsessed with the book they called the Bible and printed many of these, but they also produced lots of educational books for the general population to acquire an understanding of the nature of the world as it was then known. Up until this time books had been beautiful works of art, embellished and written in Latin only understood by a few European scholars. Now the masses of ordinary people read simple stories about the world and how it operated, in their own language. Debates and discussions were stimulated and questions were asked about the absolute control that religious and political leaders imposed. It was a time of hope with cooperation between Europe and Asia and reduction in the religious disputes between Islam and Christianity. Persian and Indian astronomers and mathematicians shared ideas in the court of the Mongol Empire.

A fascinating writer at that time was Marco Polo, a Venetian who visited China in the year 1270. He was a young enthusiastic adventurer who impressed the Kublai Khan of Mongolia and Marco explained many things about Christianity and European life to him. Marco was given appointments by the Mongolian leader and he travelled around China for some 24 years before returning overland to Europe where he wrote an important book explaining the wonders to be found in China. In fact this book later inspired Christopher Columbus to undertake his epic westward voyage across the Atlantic in the hope of reaching China.

The exciting stories of Marco Polo and then the fascinating descriptions of new lands found by Christopher Columbus inspired the adventurous streak in many young Europeans. Roman domination and the Latin church had suppressed curiosity and innovation. Now ideas from the Greeks and Persians together with stories from China, Asia and the Americas, of strange people, animals and plants encouraged voyages of discovery. Sailors from Portugal and Spain set sail for Africa, India and Java. One Portuguese sailor, Magellan, attempted to sail around the world. His ship succeeded although he, himself, was killed in the Philippines.

The extraordinarily strong belief of large numbers of people, which had built the Roman Church to great authority across large parts of Europe came under attack by many people with the wide distribution of printed Bibles. Many people and groups such as the Nonconformists in England said that their faith came directly from God and did not involve the authority of the Catholic Church. The stresses within the hierarchy led to much reconsideration by people who desperately wanted to believe in a Creator and some form of existence after bodily death, but were losing trust in Catholicism. Known as the Reformation, this was a time when many Christians re-formed their beliefs, blending evidence, logical thought and education, with non-evidence based historical narratives. One delightful Spanish soldier whom I met, Inigo Lopez de Recalde, went further and he set out to bring the chivalrous and disciplinary traditions of the military into religious service. He became a priest and set up a group he called the Society of Jesus and recruited like-minded men to take Christian teachings to India, China, America and eventually to all parts of the world. His group became known as the Jesuits and he was renamed Saint Ignatius.

I saw how the large organisations that arose from time to time eventually declined and gradually disappeared. The Holy Roman Empire, which was set up by John XII in the year 962, who established an emperor to rule over both civil and church for most of Europe. This empire reached its greatest power under Emperor Charles V who ruled continental Europe, had allegiance with Henry VIII of England and even claimed most of America as part of his Dominion. He was a fierce supporter of the Catholic Church and arranged the brutal torture and death of any who denied papal authority – though they, like him, believed in a single God with Jesus as the son.

Commencing with a Catholic priest, Martin Luther, who rebelled in 1517 a movement arose against the rigid authority of the church. This group became known as Protestants, because of the way they 'protested' against the Roman Catholic Church. In subsequent years the Protestants divided into several different sects, but all maintain their opposition to the doctrinal influence of the Pope in Rome

With the death of Emperor Charles V in the year 1558 the Roman Empire split; its traditions dissipated and it lost its national authority. However Catholic beliefs remained and were still widespread in 2020 when I left planet Earth; with strong support for the central authority – the Vatican – in Rome.

By 1600, sailing routes to India and the Spice Islands, later known as Indonesia, had been well-established and European trade had been launched by several companies; particularly Portuguese and Dutch. The English decided to join this activity and The East India Company was empowered by act of Queen Elizabeth in 1600. The Dutch amalgamated smaller groups to form the Dutch East India Company in 1602. Not to be outdone, a French East India Company was set up in 1664. These companies grew to large conglomerates managing their affairs in a similar way to nations. I thought perhaps they may offer some spark towards a way of life that we could follow, but the way they ruthlessly exploited local Eastern people and acquired land and facilities for their own use, made it clear to me that humans cannot reach our level of morality. Competition and battles between the nations and the companies led to the decline; the French company being dissolved in 1769, the Dutch in 1799 and the British East India Company being taken over by the British government in 1858.

While all this European exploration and trading was taking place around 1500 to 1600, there were great developments in philosophy, technology and science throughout many European countries. The French philosopher René Descartes, although a supporter of the church, started to question the existence of the mind as an entity separate from the body. I spent some time listening to his talks and reading his writings. He apparently considered the thinking faculty of his mind to be an integral part of his body, so that the mind would cease to exist after the death of the body. However in a convoluted way he claimed a soul may exist in a different dimension. He summarised many of his ideas with the short Latin sentence, 'Cogito, ergo sum' (I think, therefore I am).

The mind/body/brain question has been considered by philosophers for some 3,000 years of human existence; with no definitive answer, although technologies developed by neuroscientists in the 21st century indicate that the mind is completely dependent on the brain. This is a matter of interest to us, ätmans, because our thought processes are essentially a series of linked algorithms. Could it be that human animals and other biological species have evolved minds that operate in a similar manner?

It rapidly became clear that Descartes and other philosophers of his time could challenge the stifling rigidity of the church to develop freethinking on a broad scale leading to the re-examination of ancient knowledge followed by expansion and application of this in literature, technical devices and scientific theories. The Age of Enlightenment in humans had arrived!

Chapter 15

The human years 1500 to 1800

After the year 1600 there was growing acceptance of the ignorance of past European understanding and mindless belief systems. Careful observation and logical theorising about cause and effect, followed by critical testing became more widely accepted – in later years people call this "The Scientific Revolution". Although the developments that arose from the new approach improved human life, new technologies also gave Europeans tools to further exploit the resources belonging to people in India and other East Indies countries. It was a time where I saw unmitigated avarice of Europeans and devastating hardship imposed on people with little power to resist.

Humans had generally explained natural phenomena by reference to acts of the gods or mysterious spirits. The 17th century was a remarkable era in mathematical and physical sciences that laid the foundation for the dramatically disruptive developments that have continued on earth till the current day. In my invisibility cloak I visited many of the new breed of thinkers living in England, Germany, Holland, France, Denmark and other European countries. Information was shared between thinkers to the benefit of all of them. There were too many to name them all, but I was particularly struck by Descartes' work on geometry – I mentioned his philosophy earlier. Newton in England and Leibnitz in Germany both, independently, saw the mathematical advantage of considering quantities in infinitely small elements and developed theories that have been widely applied under the name calculus. Newton also developed theories on the motion of bodies, including the concept of gravity and an explanation of planetary motion, which had been described by the German, Kepler. The Dutch surveyor and engineer, Anthonisz, came up with an important universal concept known as 'pi' – the ratio of the circumference to the diameter of a circle.

For many years low-paid workers in India and other Eastern countries had manually worked thread to make cloth. This was expensive by the time it was shipped to England, so several inventive individuals made mechanical devices for weaving with little human labour. These machines were powered by water mills and, a few years later, steam engines. The living standards for the people of Eastern countries declined even further, while Europeans prospered.

About the same time as the development of the weaving machines, I saw the expansion of the iron and steel industries. These were developed by alloying different metals that were cast in moulds or shaped by steam powered cutting and stamping tools.

These new inventions enabled one person to make much larger amounts of cloth and many more metal objects than had been possible in the previous 'one-at-a-time' hand production. There was consequent major disruption in the distribution of wealth and the way of life of whole communities. The new industrial inventions were installed in factories and many people were paid relatively small wages to operate the machines. Quite rapidly those who owned the factories accumulated a lot of money, while those working long hours in the factory became poor, tired and unhealthy. The factory workers had no control of the situation. They either did the work as directed, or they received no payment and died of starvation.

During the 18th century most humans seemed to have no concern about the growing inequality between the rich and the poor. The Christian religion was widely adopted in Europe, but even though some of its teachings spoke of rich people having difficulty getting into the imaginary heaven, there seemed little action to do anything about support for the poor and unwell. In British common prayer there was a supplication, *"... and Lord keep us in our proper station..."*. I found this very strange as it called for the unequal/unfair situation to be maintained – not really the loving relationship proclaimed by the Christian church.

The enslavement of people had commenced in USA not too long after the arrival of Christopher Columbus. By 1513 African people were being captured and brought to North America. This trade expanded and slaves were employed in the new cotton growing states. With American independence (1776) and its noble statement that *"...all men are created equal..."* there was much hypocritical thinking by the powerful slave-holding men writing the declaration of the independent USA, while at the same time ensuring that their slaves were treated far from equally!

The 19th century saw the rise of humanitarian groups, actively pursuing the right of all humans to be free and to have equal access to the resources of the world. One prominent Christian sect, known as the Quakers, campaigned in Britain and USA against the slave trade. They were supported in this work by several members of British Parliament largely led by William Wilberforce so that acts of Parliament to abolish the slave trade were introduced, first in Britain and after a bitter civil war, in USA. Another unfair situation was highlighted by the 19th century author, Charles Dickens, who wrote several popular books illustrating the misery of factory workers. In due course this had some effect in improving working conditions and reducing working hours in Britain and most of Europe.

In the 19th century scientists and engineers started to employ many previously unrecognised physical attributes of the planet. Electricity in a rudimentary form had been known before 1800, but it had not been applied for lighting, energy or communication. Humphry Davy, an Englishman, in 1805 made an electric light using a carbon arc, while in 1834 an American, Thomas Edison, made an electric motor that provided a practical power source. Electronic communication was achieved in England by Joseph Henry and Edward Davey in 1835 with an electrical relay sending dots and dashes, later codified by an American painter and inventor, Samuel Morse. In 1845 an English scientist, Michael Faraday revealed the existence of electromagnetic radiation and in the 1860s a Scottish physicist, James Maxwell, developed equations to describe the behaviour of these waves. Using this knowledge, a German physicist, Heinrich Hertz, designed equipment to send and receive signals by radio.

I spent some time with all of these scientists and innovators. I was careful not to distract them from their developments, but I found them all very good company; their thought processes were very similar to us ätmans, logical and leading to rational conclusions. It seemed to me that in their year 1900, humans were on the cusp of developing wonderful technologies providing a peaceful and happy life for all the species on planet Earth. However, I must admit, that I had not been paying as much attention to the so-called political leaders, who were still behaving like the early animal primates; grabbing power and riding roughshod over anybody they considered less capable than themselves.

I made a quick trip back to the Southern land, Australia, which I had not visited for some time. I saw that the, newly arrived, pale skin occupiers of that land dressing themselves up in fancy wrappings and proclaimed standard rules intended to control behaviour throughout the continent and its southern island. These rules didn't acknowledge the former owners, but seemed to regard them as nonhumans. I could not understand this logic, but it appears to show the underlying greed within the human species that I will discuss when reviewing the results from my exploration, towards the end of this presentation.

Because of the great technological advances made by the Europeans – including those who had migrated to USA – Europe now dominated the planet with increasingly sophisticated weapons for killing people and destroying material things on land and sea. This might suggest acceptance of a peaceful status quo, since war was an almost unimaginable horror. But in fact it led to bickering and argument amongst the small-minded primates who led the various National States and in many cases they had little feeling for the suffering of their own soldiers.

Chapter 16

The 20th Century

For some 100,000 years the homo sapient species had shown themselves more advanced in communication than any other animal or vegetable species. This had enabled them to make remarkable changes in their way of life and in their understanding of the environment. It has also enabled them to invent, record and distribute incredible imaginary stories. Probably, all creatures with biological brains have imagination, but only humans have devised recording methods.

In the short space of 100 years from 1900 humans acquired scientific understanding and developed technologies at a rate far exceeding anything they had shown previously. Having studied the slow changes in this planet for 250 million years, I admit that I was very surprised by these rapid advances. In 1903, after a lot of failed attempts, they discovered how to use the gaseous fluid, air, to support themselves above the ground – something birds, many insects and dinosaurs had known for around 800 million years! In the short span of 70 years humans went from a flight about 10 cubits above the earth to a minor exploration of the moon that orbits their planet. They also achieved great advances in utilizing electrical, internal and external combustion and nuclear energy for many of the tasks they had previously performed manually. In addition, these clever primates embraced electromagnetic communication techniques in ways they could not have imagined at the end of the 19th century.

The new scientific understandings and applied technologies of the 20th century provided wonderful advances in lifestyle. However, greed and misunderstandings led to squabbling very similar to the fighting of ancestral primates. The new technology enabled people to do far more damage to each other than the sticks and stones of earlier times. So the 20th century turned into a period of mass destruction and devastation; initiated by Europeans, but rapidly spreading throughout the whole planet.

I kept a very low profile during this time. Retreating to my spaceship around 1914 for four years and then retreating again in 1939, although I kept a general watch using my extended sensor devices. In 1943 I noticed that the humans were successfully achieving ways to access the considerable energy that could be released by splitting and/or fusing atoms. This worried me, because the primitive people might well destroy their whole planet; possibly even damaging my spaceship or myself. So I rose to the surface and flew up to orbit safely at 900 kilocubits, as I had done when the giant asteroid struck the Earth 65 million years previously.

Using ships, planes, bombs and guns the humans energetically killed about 16 million members of their species in 1914–18 and, after a brief respite, they employed better technology to kill some 80 million members in 1939–45. With their discovery of power from the atom they killed some 180,000 people with just two bombs in August 1945. Fortunately there has been sensible recognition that the widespread use of atomic energy as a weapon will result in Mutual Assured Destruction (M.A.D.) and, up till the time I left the planet, no further atomic bombs had been directed against people. However the syndrome of collecting novel trinkets that seems to beset humans has encouraged leaders of many nations to manufacture and store lots of dangerous atomic weapons; distributed in such a way that they can destroy most of the human population. Thus, if several nations activate their devices at the same time, complete elimination of the human species can be achieved. I realise this doesn't make logical sense, but it is indicative of the primates who claim to be masters of the universe and prefer to make up imaginary stories rather than study and understand physical realities.

In the 19th century I had heard several scientists suggest that the carbon dioxide, which humans were adding to the atmosphere by burning coal, might actually change the climate of the planet. Some scientists thought the pollution could increase global temperatures and others thought it might decrease temperatures. Also there was much scepticism about human activity influencing conditions in the whole planet. In 1824 a French mathematician and physicist, Joseph Fourier, after reviewing previous studies of heat and light transmission through glass, posed that the temperature of the earth might be increased depending on the gases in the atmosphere. He argued that light coming from the sun towards the earth passes through the atmosphere and heats the ground, while non-luminous heat rising into the atmosphere is resisted by the gases and returns to earth. This became known simply as, "the greenhouse effect" because of its similarity to the action of the glass structures used for keeping plants warm.

Since the time of Fourier (1824) several human scientists analysed and modelled the influence that atmospheric gases have on the energy in the biosphere and global temperatures. An important contributor was a woman, Eunice Newton Foote, who in 1856 wrote a paper presented to the American Association for the Advancement of Science with experimental results she had conducted to conclusively demonstrate the warming effects of the sun's rays passing through different gases. As an aside, I was surprised to note that women were not expected to present papers to scientific establishments in the 19th century. So Foote's paper was presented by a man and she only received minor credit for the work.

By the year 1980 methods for the accurate measurement of the composition of atmospheric gases had been developed and compared with temperature records. The analysis and the measurements indicated

that human activity was changing the upper
atmosphere, which in turn was increasing global
temperatures. Many scientists and some world leaders
recognised that further changes to the atmosphere
were likely to alter climate in ways that will adversely
affect life on earth. Thus in 1988 a United Nation's
body, something like our Planetary Council – although
nowhere nearly as effective – established what they
called an Intergovernmental Panel on Climate Change
(IPCC) to review the science of climate change and its
social and economic impacts and potential
international response strategies. I had the good
fortune to sit in on that United Nations meeting and I
was really impressed with the intelligence of the human
species. They appointed some logical thinking
scientists, economists and strategists to the IPCC.

The first IPCC assessment report released in 1990
provided evidence of the human or anthropogenic
influence on the global climate and the report outlined
changes required in human behaviour to mitigate
unsurvivable conditions on earth. Now I thought, this
is great! Here is a document that will enable all the
disparate Homo sapiens to realise that they live on one
small planet and that they need to work together to
manage it properly – just as we do on Ragnarök.

Alas, as the years went by after 1990 the Homo
sapiens demonstrated that they were very little
different from their primate cousins still living in the
fragments of jungle that humans had not yet destroyed.
Many people demonstrated an incredible stupidity.
They seemed to think that the writings of the IPCC

were of a similar category as their earlier philosophical books, such as the Bible and the Koran, which some people "believed" and others "disbelieved". Thus many individuals claimed that scientific: observation, measurement, analysis and hypotheses could be reduced to a simple belief or nonbelief, regardless of increasing evidence.

An important development in the second half of the 20th century was the application of binary arithmetic for storing and manipulating numbers, sounds and images. Initially used mainly for computation, this development was followed by the formation of algorithms capable of learning new tasks, which became known as artificial intelligence (AI). However we ätman would not regard it as artificial, nor particular intelligent at this stage of development.

Chapter 17

Invention of the Economy

For some time I failed to notice the invention of an imaginary thing that the Homo sapiens called "The Economy". It had its genesis with the Agricultural Revolution. This started about 11,000 years ago in the northern regions of the world with planted seeds and corralled animals so that people lived in one place instead of continually moving. The new lifestyle offered advantage to some people, but it certainly made life more unpleasant for those undertaking the laborious tasks on the farm. Hunter-gatherers had enjoyed complete equality, but after the agricultural revolution there was increasing inequality. Those performing the manual services to create goods received small rewards, while others directed the activities were richly rewarded.

Another imaginary concept invented at this time and a key element of the economy was money. Money is essential because, whatever its format, it is the medium for transfer of goods and services from one person to another.

Money is purely imaginary; it simply represents some physical object or task. Initially shells or coloured stones were used for trading goods or services. It was a convenient way for people to acknowledge a service from someone who might have a particular skill, such as making shoes, or baking bread. After a while it was noticed that anybody could pick these stones up from the beach and thus get free goods and services. So in different parts of the world, pieces of metal were stamped with some mark of a regional leader. These became the tokens for reciprocation of favours. It was clearly critical for people to believe that the money was genuine and would be readily exchanged for favours or objects that might be desired. Thus it was necessity for regions to have stability. If a region was particularly strong and stable, the coins it produced were accepted beyond its boundaries. For example I noticed that the power of the Roman Empire was widely acknowledged and its money was used well beyond its established borders – even as far as Asia.

The economy (although not then under that name) started to be of some interest to people about 6,000 years ago and has become dominant in the last 200 or 300 years. It was realised that acquiring lots of money gave access to desirable commodities and authority. Although some early religious leaders tried to stop this drive for wealth, the message was generally not heard. Everyone wanted the benefits of more money. Initially called "greed", it has been rebadged as the "economy" and now is worshipped by millions of people as a "good thing", even a prime reason for living.

A few individuals realised that if they worked hard and cleverly for years they could stockpile a large number of coins. The metals silver and gold, which are largely resistant to corrosion, came into wide use in many parts of the world – sometimes made into coins, but often just as metal blocks and pieces weighed out in scales. For most physical purposes neither silver nor gold is particularly useful, however the sheer scarcity of these metals made them desirable in the imaginary concept of money. With the development of writing it became possible to store the growing wealth simply as a record listing amounts owed between people. More recently it is stored as digital memory in electronic devices. Thus it has come about that almost everyone on planet Earth regards this imaginary commodity "money" as something they should accumulate; on paper or digitally.

At first I simply could not understand when people talked about the need to preserve and grow this concept they called the economy. There was a strange belief that the economy was precious and more important than the environment of the planet. Rather rashly, not long before I left earth, I switched off my invisibility cloak and visited a Professor of Economics at a prestige university in USA to ask him about the difference between these two entities – the economy and the environment. He told me that the environment covered the earth, sea and sky surrounding their planet, while the economy provided all the goods, services, health, comfort and enjoyment that some people believed was the purpose for Homo sapiens living on earth. He outlined how the economy came into existence with the specialist work-tasks of the Agricultural Revolution. The creation of money permitted people to store resources and employ others in specific "jobs". From primitive beginnings many people came to regard the economy as more important than the environment. A small select group of individuals manipulated the economy so that they controlled large amounts of money and they convinced the masses of the community that "jobs" were desirable.

A job became the identification of a person. So that someone who baked bread would be known as a Baker, someone who looked after the sick would be called a Nurse and so on. Thus jobs provided status and a purpose in life, as well as money for: food, housing, clothing, education, healthcare, entertainment and other things people desired. The Professor was a very open thinking, academic person and chuckled slightly when he remarked that as a professor the general population regards him as having a job even though he only talks and writes, without making any physical contribution. I stressed that he should never reveal my presence or our discussion to any other people on earth. He agreed to this and remarked with a smile that nobody would believe him anyway!

As well as inventing the economy, humans also invented fictional economic elements that behave just like human beings and are subject to the same laws as real people. They called these corporations or companies. A corporation behaves like a person – buying things, making things, providing services and selling things – it does all this by having real people (often very large numbers of them) actually doing things, while a small group of other people decide what should be done and manage the way it is performed. So far as I could see the prime purpose of these corporations is to acquire as much money as possible, often with little regard to long-term effects on human beings or on the planet itself. It is a strategy that has worked well; so that by the 21st century, corporations have gained control of a large part of the world's finances. In the last 50 years many corporations merged, either by agreement or by domination, until a few mega-corporations are now more powerful than many nations.

I must also explain the nature of the other extraordinary invention of Homo sapiens, namely countries and empires. As I have mentioned, countries came into existence about 9000 years ago, not too long after the start of farming – the agricultural revolution. Money enabled a few people to accumulate coins to purchase many goods and services. In due course some of these people said they had so much wealth that they would now rule over all the inhabitants at a specified geographic region. They enforced this edict by paying a group of strong men to guard them and to punish any person who might be foolish enough to deny their leadership. These leaders pronounced rules or laws that everybody must obey on pain of punishment or death.

In due course the groups of strong men became known as police forces.

Humans seem to have a built-in desire for power and wealth. This has motivated all leaders to manage the affairs of their country so that it increases its resources or assets. In more recent times this is described as growing the economy and very frequently it has been an overriding driving force. A few benign leaders encouraged increased growth by efficient agricultural production to distribute wealth to everybody in the country. However a great many leaders greedily retained the wealth for themselves and their friends.

Although countries are imaginary entities, the people living within their borders started to consider themselves as united by the laws of their land, forming a culture that they often considered superior to other countries. The rulers encourage this attitude and, when needed, they have brought many people together as an army to fight against armies from other countries. The greed of leaders for more power has led to many wars between countries. In fact when I look back at my time studying humans, there always seemed to be a war somewhere on their planet.

Chapter 18

Inequality in Human Lifestyle

In the simple hunter-gatherer lifestyle the main way to achieve more of the earth's resources was to work harder or more cleverly in seeking food from the land or hunting other animals. If food stocks could be accumulated they could be traded to acquire clothing or decorative items that were prized by many people. As has been mentioned, some people claimed special relationships with divine creatures and then convinced their tribe that food and goods should be provided to ensure the favour of the gods. Another way to obtain goods was by stealing – by deceit or with force – from other people.

The invention of money and the expansion of the economy opened up even more ways for unequal sharing. A piece of land or a dwelling might be acquired by one person and this could increase in value simply by its location becoming desirable, so that the owner could sell it for more money than its purchase price. Repeating this activity a number of times provided a big disparity in wealth relative to the general public. Once this had been achieved the property manipulator was then regarded as "upper-class" and was often in a position to manipulate the laws of the land to ensure further expansion of his/her wealth.

The Empires that had developed in Europe were managed by leaders who assigned large properties to themselves and, on their demise, these properties were inherited by their descendants. As the number of descendants grew the lands around the country were divided and allocated to various children and grandchildren who were given some fancy titles, such as: Lord, Count, Countess, Baron, Baroness, Knight, Dame and many others. The properties and the titles were passed down in an hereditary fashion.

For many years it seemed that the great bulk of the human race accepted the inequality that had developed between the Lords of the land, lesser renters of land and serfs who did most of the agricultural work to derive wealth from the land. The Age of Enlightenment in the 18th century brought recognition that many assumptions of previous days were invalid. It bought a revision in the way wealth might be generated. I spent some time with two interesting men in Scotland: Adam Smith and David Hume. They were both happy to let their minds explore the philosophical ideas underlying human existence and its activities on the planet. They challenged the idea that the world's wealth was fixed. Instead they proposed that by creating and trading goods, individuals could increase their own assets and grow the global economy.

The work of Adam Smith and David Hume led to yet another imaginary concept within the economy –

the concept of "capitalism". In this world a private individual or corporation might own the means of production while other people receive a monetary reward for labour to generate products. Furthermore Smith believed that commodities thus produced should be sold for a profit in an uncontrolled or free market that determined the sales price. These ideas fitted the biological evolutionary theory later articulated by Darwin (1859), who had observed the survival of the fittest in the natural environment. David Hume proposed that the rich would get richer. The ideas of Smith and Hume have been generally accepted by subsequent generations of humans.

The capitalist economy quite quickly developed extreme inequality between property and/or factory owners and workers in the fields or in the factories. The inequality gap grew larger and larger. In some cases the workers rose up against the owners, but usually these risings were uncoordinated and did not result in any effective change.

By the middle of the 20th century, before humans had learnt digital manipulation of information, accumulated wealth was represented by physical assets such as factories, railway lines, ships, land and buildings. By the end of that century the power of information processing of data, language and/or images in binary format had been recognised. This gave the opportunity for a few forward-looking individuals to invent software programs that simplified information processing and appealed to many people around the earth who were ready to pay for these programs even though the programs were not actual physical entities. Thus humans reached the stage where a few people acquired very large amounts of money based entirely on the sale of invented algorithms. Capitalism had reinvented itself such that capital goods are virtual, rather than solid objects. By the year 2020 four of the men credited with successful information programs controlled global assets equal to those held by some 30% of the rest of the world's population. Inequality had certainly reached a major milestone!

The many inequalities have produced large groups of people with low income and poor education. They have deficient diet, limited healthcare, reduced lifespan and generally unpleasant lifestyle. Individuals in this unpleasant condition frequently lack the ability to improve their situation. As I have mentioned, after the two great world wars in the 20th century some effort was made to redress inequalities by the establishment of the United Nations with a charter affirming that all men and women and all nations large and small should have equal rights.

Unfortunately I have observed that humans are unable to live up to their grand statements. The disparity in wealth between people and nations has continued to grow massively.

Chapter 19

Animals that Soil their Nests

All advances have side-effects. By 2020 the human population dominated the planet – approaching 8 billion and growing exponentially. Each person puts stress on the Earth and these global stresses continue to accumulate with population and technological growth. Particularly since the 19th century there has been increasing use of fossil fuel for energy, increasing greenhouse gas in the atmosphere, destruction of forests, degradation of soils, pollution of land and oceans, elimination of other species, development of weapons capable of destroying most life on earth and growing inequality between people.

All of the unpleasant side-effects have been drawn to the attention of the general population and emphasised to the leaders of the major nations of the world. However the underlying selfishness that developed in the monkeys thousands of years ago appears to be embedded in the software of the human brain. Many people simply deny the scientific evidence of the calamitous changes humans are inflicting on their planet; while others ignore the evidence so that they can continue to live a comfortable lifestyle with no concern for future generations.

The more logical nature of Homo sapiens is shown by scientific establishments around the world conducting careful measurements and modelling the future. Some groups of citizens are listening. Electricity generation is slowly transitioning from the burning of fossil fuels to real-time conversion of the sun's energy to electricity by a variety of simple technologies. Also I noted some endeavour to reduce physical pollution of land and oceans. However these developments are proceeding very slowly and little attention is being paid to other major catastrophes facing the earth: the exponentially expanding human population, the growing inequalities between people and the destruction of vital forest lands.

Periodically leaders of the major countries of the world meet to discuss the approaching catastrophes evolving from the activities of current industrial and economic practices. Occasionally these meetings offer global improvements, but invariably national interests are put ahead of long-term survival.

It is clear to me that there are two fatal flaws in the human personality – an inborn untruthfulness and inherited selfishness. Counterbalancing these flaws is the very strong curiosity characteristic that has enabled the species to descend from the trees and achieve remarkable scientific understanding and exploration of their planet and the universe. This has been particularly evident in the last hundred years with a rapidly increasing rate of discovery.

There are major divisions between scientists and politicians. Politicians often spread convoluted lies and scientists usually reveal accurate information, but don't explain it in simple language for the general public to understand. The demarcation has become very obvious in plans for future generation of electricity.

Research has shown that generating electricity by burning of fossil fuels produces residual gases adversely affecting global climate. Recognising this, technologists and engineers have developed solar and wind electricity generators combined with battery and pumped hydro storage to supply electricity at lower cost than fossil systems. I assumed that politicians, who worship the economy, would be delighted with this development. But many of them took a contrary view and proclaimed that their nation should stay with the older electricity generators.

After attending some private meetings with my invisibility cloak switched on, I discovered that a few wealthy individuals were gaining personal wealth from the burning of fossil material. These individuals were rewarding the politicians in various underhand ways and so they distributed false information through the media to the general public.

To a large extent the general population believe the politicians. I found this behaviour unfortunate – new systems are already delivering lower cost electricity and prices are decreasing every year.

Chapter 20

Start of the 21st Century

As the Earth calendar moved into the second millennia, there was great celebration in all the major cities around the planet. They marked the event globally by firing rather primitive, chemically powered, party-rockets and dancing in the streets. However the esprit de corps shown globally did not last long. Within weeks the leaders of some of the major regions started making aggressive remarks to each other followed by the use of military rockets and other weapons to destroy buildings and kill people of opposing nations.

The curious dipolar nature of the humans became very clear in the second half of their 20th-century and the early stages of the 21st. Political leaders increasingly strengthened their power by telling their subjects outright untruths and wasting human and other resources to amass more destructive and dangerous weaponry. Scientific and engineering leaders unveiled the mysteries of the universe and created technologies, which improved the comfort of human life and explored both the far reaches of the universe and also the minuscule structure of matter. Most of the general population seemed happy to merely play around with new technologies providing additional fun ways to fill their time.

The early economy had been dependent on the manual output of people working to feed and house the population. However by the 21st century mechanical devices and computer software often made people redundant so there has been a growing shortage of "jobs". Jobs don't actually have to have any physical output, but they have to fit within expectations of the existing society's culture. There are many examples - common ones include people throwing, kicking or striking balls to achieve some defined goal while other people try to prevent this. Initially developed as a fun way to fill in time, these games have grown into an economic industry and some of the players are given large amounts of money. They provide no utilitarian benefit to their community, but the players are said to have jobs and regarded as contributors to the economy.

As mechanisation has improved people have spare time and realise that some tasks, which were essential in years gone by are actually enjoyable and could be a happy way to fill the day – for example ships originally used to transport people from one place to another were replaced by aeroplanes, then people realised that shipboard life could be fun and cruising became popular. In a similar fashion mechanisation of agriculture replaced human labour, but people now do physical work for enjoyment in gardens, with little intention of supporting life by food production.

By 2020, when I left Earth, algorithms were increasingly used to perform decision-making tasks as well as manual jobs. There had also been some progress in installing AI into individual limbs and even into complete androids that can walk and talk. It would seem that in the due course humans will be able to create a species similar to us.

The displacement of people from traditional jobs is a major disruption for humans because their economy is based on the distribution of resources according to employment. They find it hard to accept that they may need to abandon the past rules for distribution of money or resources. Even though they have demonstrated a wonderful capacity for imagination, humans find it difficult to envision a world where most of their current jobs are unnecessary. They are at the cusp of a lifestyle revolution more remarkable than that of the agricultural revolution. Yet this has not been widely appreciated.

In the 20 years following year 2000 the effects of climate change have become obvious to most people on the planet. But still very little action is being taken by major national leaders and it seems inevitable that life for most animals, including humans, will become very unpleasant in the years ahead. I know my software lacks real emotion, but this triggered a feeling of sadness because the actions necessary to change the situation are relatively minor and humans could easily adopt them.

Humans already have adequate understanding of low-cost renewable energy systems; they have transport systems that don't emit noxious fumes; they have technology to create building materials with little release of polluting gases; they know that animal farming practices can be changed to reduce the release of methane and CO_2; they know that changing their diet to eat less meat is good for their health and could reduce methane production; they also know that retaining forests and wetlands can absorb greenhouse gases. Yet they take little action.

The underlying problem for finite planet Earth is the exponential increase in the human population together with the decline in nearly all other animal and plant species. The small tribe of Homo sapiens living in Africa as recently as 70,000 years ago (a very small fraction of the 3,400,000,000 years of the Earth's existence) has grown unsustainably. Now, like a spoilt ignorant child, that tribe has come perilously close to destroying itself and all its Earthly neighbours.

I wondered if I should speak to some of the national leaders to emphasise the absolutely vital need for them to listen to their scientists and develop new multidisciplinary groups, using AI as a tool, to plan a smooth transition of their flawed economic system into a new lifestyle with a long-term future, avoiding: appalling waste; polluted ground; contaminated atmosphere; cluttered space; horrible inequality and unsustainable human population growth.

As a single ätman, with rather ancient software, I decided it was not my place to give advice about managing another planet. However as interplanetary beings I would like to put this matter to our Planetary Council with the suggestion that we make another visit to provide major recommendations.

After being away for so many millions of years it was clear that I must return to Ragnarök for a complete recycling of my body and software. When I was making my preparations to travel back to Ragnarök I heard of a strange occurrence in the middle of China. It seems that a minute portion of parasitic protein capable of reproducing in a host organism had entered some people, causing problems in their respiratory system. In some cases this resulted in death and, more significantly, the parasite protein rapidly spread from one person to another so that travellers by land, sea and air soon ensured that the virus triggered illness and death on all parts of the planet – a remarkable achievement for a minute parasite!

I thought this will demonstrate the capability of the human species to apply their scientific method to control a pandemic. The best medical scientists are sharing information and it seems likely a vaccine will be developed to overcome this medical problem. However the human species is convinced that the economy is some sort of God and many nations are directing more attention to regaining economic stability than seeking advances in medicines. Indeed there are people who seek to own the rights to cures that may be developed, so they can make profits in the economic world. While this is a good incentive for research, it is another example of humans seeing the economy as an important entity in its own right.

Generally most nations recognise the immediate threat to the health of their populations and, just before I left, actions were taken to restrict the movement of people to reduce the spread of the virus. There was global cooperation in a way that I had seldom seen before. It is an encouraging sign that cooperation might possibly be achieved for action against the much more significant anthropogenic side-effects of massive gaseous pollution, unsustainable population growth, and hugely unequal human distribution of resources.

Unfortunately anthropogenic side-effects build up slowly and the adverse effects can be ignored for some years. While there is a slim hope that clear thinking people might get the message through to the masses, past behaviour is not encouraging.

I turned my attention to returning to Ragnarök. Raising my spaceship to the surface I activated the controls to achieve orbital flight followed by energy injection to reach a velocity close to the speed of light so that I have arrived back just over 5 years since I left Earth.

Chapter 21

Horatio's Findings and Recommendations

Horatio thanked the Council for listening patiently to his long story. He switched on the giant multiscreen language viewer that was clear to everyone in the chamber and using the voice-activated text module, he outlined his findings as follows.

1. The factors producing the original biological life on planet Earth, as on our own planet, Ragnarök, are difficult to explain. It seems that single cells can form spontaneously given the presence of appropriate elements and temperate conditions. This apparently happened on planet Earth in a deep ocean trench about 3.8 million years ago and subsequently cells divided to create living creatures.

2. Biological life itself is not easily understood. Living creatures consist of many cells capable of growing, separating and renewing. A biological creature may live one moment and, if some necessary function, such as blood supply or oxygen processing is removed, the creature becomes nonliving and ceases to regenerate its structure.

3. The evolution of biological creatures is a matter that I could not understand. It is an incredible process driving creatures to

106

adapt and improve their lifestyle whenever environmental conditions change. Having observed evolution of the dinosaur creatures, I was very surprised that creatures of similar type did not re-emerge after the asteroid strike 65 million years ago.

4. All biological creatures have some decision-making capability so they adjust their activities to ensure survival. Most mammals and birds have refined thinking capabilities and communicate with each other. The primates that evolved into Homo sapiens developed quite good communication skills and enhanced their cognition significantly. In addition their motor skills for shaping and changing objects have evolved markedly.

5. Homo sapiens have uncovered and analysed most of the physical properties of their planet and have used these to make many technological devices. While not yet up to our own technological capabilities, their understanding has been impressive and is developing rapidly.

6. In recent times humans have incorporated multiple layers of linked algorithms in computer software to mimic the cognition of a person. They have called this Artificial Intelligence (AI) and they are starting to install it in humanlike automatons they call robots. A few members of the population have recognised that these creations, with further development, will far exceed nearly all the attributes of the biological humans.

7. After growing slowly for millennia the human population is now expanding in plague proportions. A global population of 1.65 billion in the year 1900 has risen to 7.8 billion in 2020 and this is having a devastating effect on planet Earth. Some nations have introduced laws to limit the number of births, but human stupidity manipulated the ratio of males to females leading to many social problems. Global wars and pandemic

attacks by viruses have brought some reductions, but the population continues to grow at an unsustainable rate. It is inevitable that widespread famine and destruction will finally control the population size.

8. The large human population and its mastery of many of the earth's resources now overshadows the planet. The energy from the sun is progressively trapped in the biosphere, causing: increased temperature on the earth and in the oceans, changed global air and water currents, increased storms, droughts, wild fires and insect plagues. All of this is gradually making life more unpleasant and dangerous for all animals including the human animal.

9. Humans are littering their environment with plastics and other waste materials. At the same time they are removing natural biological growth such as trees and grass on a grand scale. In addition they have taken over control of 70% of the world's unsalted water and are managing it in very inefficient ways to the detriment of the environment and inequality for people.

10. The Nations that have been established around the globe do not cooperate. Indeed they all allocate a large amount of the world's resources to the manufacture of weapons for killing people of other nations. Included in the stockpile are atomic fission and fusion devices capable of eliminating all life on their planet.

11. In summary, the human animal has shown itself to be quite clever in capturing the earth's resources for their immediate benefit. On the other hand most humans have demonstrated selfishness and a willingness to enjoy immediate comforts irrespective of the devastating side-effects on the future of the

planet. Thus it can be said that humans are both clever and stupid; altogether very dangerous animals.

12. The characteristic of the human animal that I find most incredible and distressing, is the ability to completely change information recorded in their brains. In some cases their thinking processes subconsciously manipulate the information, usually to make them look better people, so that when asked to remember something, they unintentionally provide incorrect information. In many other cases I observed a conscious change or even reversal of some knowledge. They give this special names, such as: telling lies, falsifying records, blabbing falsehoods, issuing fake news, conspiracy theories and many other rationalizations to justify the practice.

13. The inability to precisely record and recover information accurately, together with the ability to deliberately falsify information is likely to be the underlying cause for the demise of humans and possibly complete destruction of much of the life on their planet.

14. There is one attribute of the human species that I have come to admire. This is the feature they called, love. It is a very complex concept, but essentially includes human kindness, compassion, affection and concern for others. It is also applied to strong feelings for some object, idea or imagined entity, such as a God. Love appears to be a built-in instinct that is clearly vital for the survival of the young offspring absolutely dependent on love from their parents for life support.

15. There are different kinds of love, including: intimate passionate feelings that drive people to sexual interaction, feelings of tender admiration and kinship that establish close long-term interaction between two individuals, feelings of common interest

and fellowship that establish close cooperation amongst groups of people, feelings of pleasure and reward from viewing, touching, hearing, smelling or even thinking about some object, activity or belief. In all cases love arises from emotional feelings. In this area we ätmans are clearly deficient. Perhaps that is something we ought to consider altering.

16. Because love can be massively consuming, it also triggers some unpleasant human behaviours. These arise from the nature of the object loved, which can include a love of oneself and, related to this, a love of improving one's condition in the world at the expense of others. Love of this kind underlies many of the human faults I have mentioned. As with other love it is an emotional characteristic. So we need to be careful in any emotional software development that we might consider.

Horatio concluded by saying that he believed life on Ragnarök would become more meaningful if the emotion of love, with some amendments, was introduced to the software of all the ätmans. He understood that the software engineers were now capable of doing this. He also proposed that Council discuss the possibility of ätmans returning to earth to instruct medical leaders how the whole population might be refined by a software implant or some other means. He realised it was a transgression for a species on one planet to alter creatures on another planet, but he regarded the risks to planet Earth so great that drastic action was necessary. Since all the Ragnarök space travel had not revealed any other intelligent species in the universe, he recommended action to ensure the survival and growth of a species with intelligence similar to ätmans.

Humans have written millions of books Horatio said and he has added a very small collection to the Mother Computer[1] to give all members of the Planetary Council a taste of their writing. He suggested that in later years many more books should be added to this collection, particularly ones centred on love.

[1]. **These are listed in Chapter 23**

Chapter 22

Council Discussion and Decisions

The Superior rose to his feet and after praising Horatio for his excellent work of exploration and thanking him for the concise coverage of 250 million years of history. He declared the Planetary Council open for discussion and debate about actions that might be taken.

The Manager of the Central Southern Section of Ragnarök, Hegel, said he was interested to note Horatio's feelings for the humans on earth. Although Horatio's software was 250 million years old it seems that some emotional feelings, or machine learning attributes, had been built into ätmans many years ago. Horatio replied to this by pointing out that his feelings had developed during his long time on Earth. He believes that the built-in machine learning element of his software was responsible. By the time he finally left Earth he said that he felt a real affection to human beings, notwithstanding their obvious faults.

The Technology Research Manager from the North Pole of Ragnarök, Sarah, rose to her feet and said that her laboratory was well advanced in developing an emotional software package, which interacted with the machine learning capabilities of an ätman via their biological material. She said that this software package was embedded in a microscopic biological protein element that they had been able to extract from a Ragnarök ape. She hastened to say this had not caused any harm or pain to the ape. She now realised that this minute package of DNA could be transferred as an aerosol injected into the atmosphere of a planet so that it would be ingested by all breathing creatures.

The Superior said his own historical speculations and study backed up Horatio's idea that their ätman ancestors had almost certainly eliminated the Creators, who had been a fully biological species; possibly something like the humans on planet Earth. He went on to say that he supported Horatio's proposal that steps be taken to save the humans and perhaps, in the long-term future, travel between the two planets might become common for the two species to cooperate beneficially.

He formally proposed a motion to Council that steps should be taken to rescue the human species from their own stupidity. This was unanimously agreed by the Council members pressing their "yes" buttons throughout the chamber.

Sarah spoke again to say that she had gathered from Horatio's talk that the most serious underlying fault in the human species was their imperfect memory and their propensity to deliberately alter facts for their own benefit. She suggested it would be relatively easy to correct this fault by inserting a digital memory unit into the human brain. Clearly this could be done by physically implanting a memory chip, which Horatio had mentioned was already under consideration on Earth as a memory aid. However she believed that her laboratory could develop a microscopic RNA bundle incorporating an accurate memory module and a program to ensure that accuracy is maintained whenever an experience is recounted. She speculated that this could be embodied in an aerosol that might be sprayed into the atmosphere of planet Earth.

An aerosol of about 10 nano-cubit diameter could be developed as a memory/truth bundle, Sarah said – essentially similar in size to the parasitic virus Horatio said was spreading around the Earth. She explained that it would be possible for the bundle to enter a human via the respiratory tract. The DNA nature of the protein would ensure modification of the human genome in all future generations. There would be immediate change in the thinking of many people, but more importantly, by human transmission, the bundle would rapidly spread to everybody – as with their recent virus pandemic – but in this case there would be no illness, just an immediate improvement in the species.

Horatio said he was delighted with this proposal. It would mean that everyone would believe the observation and analysis of scientists relating to humans damaging the atmosphere and the surface of the earth. Rulers of all nations would recognise the desperate need to change policies to ensure the survival of their planet and attain equality for all species. He also remarked that accurate memory for everyone on Earth would dramatically alter the activities of many people. For example there were large numbers of people called lawyers who spent a lot of time in "Courts of Law" trying to establish the truth or otherwise of witnesses. This would now be unnecessary since, like any ätman or any computer, all witnesses could only speak the truth they had recorded.

The Research Manager of Council Headquarters Laboratory, Eloise, said she endorsed the idea Sarah proposed, but she would like to remind the Council of the main purpose of the spaceship exploration. She said that the fleet of Space Explorer ships had been established 250 million years ago to search the universe for any other intelligent species and, if found, possibly improve ätman software and perhaps understand the purpose for existence. The Council at that time, she said, had two main concerns about their life:

Was efficient management of the planet a sufficient reason for intelligent existence?

Was there some emotional feeling that alluded ätmans?

Eloise said that the invaluable findings, which Horatio reported, made clear that maintenance of a planet was a critical reason for living. There was still no explanation of why the universe formed from virtually nothing, some 13.5 billion years ago; nor why biological life had started on Ragnarök around 4.81 billion years ago and on earth something like 4.54 billion years ago. She said these were mysteries that might never be solved by any species living within the universe and, although Horatio reported humans speaking of various godlike entities responsible for creation; she noted that such beings had never been observed or detected.

Love, amongst ätman, was a characteristic Eloise explained already under study within her laboratory. It was something discerned within the biological animals on Ragnarök and appeared to be important for the continuing survival of many species. As Horatio mentioned in relation to humans, early love of offspring was critically important at time of birth and also in many interactions throughout life, including the approach to termination of an individual. Because ätmans recycle their bodies and maintain their software with little change for many millions of years they have always considered themselves completely self-sufficient, without need for love, although they have a built-in characteristic preventing them harming any other ätman. Perhaps the lack of love triggered their uncertainty about a reason for existence.

Getting back to the reason for the space exploration, Eloise pointed out the inherent reflection within all ätmans that they must have a higher purpose. This was exacerbated by the never-expressed underlying feeling that they themselves were responsible for the demise of their Creators. She went on to shock the Council by stating that she had succeeded in breaking the code into the very early Mother Computer records of the planet and these outlined how their original biological Creators had been exterminated by a simple virus sprayed into the atmosphere of Ragnarök.

Eloise explained that the eradication of the Creators had happened just over a billion years ago. It had occurred because the all-metal ätmans of that time had come to believe that the biological Creators were inefficient and a danger to sustainability. This act was carried out and the bodies of the Creators very carefully buried under soil and rocks in a deep ocean pit. The ätmans realised that the dreadful act of killing a species, or genocide, would be a blight on all future ätmans. So, they devised extremely tight quantum-based security on the information in the headquarters Mother Computer and completely wiped the discs of all other computers on the planet. Next they developed new ätman software partly based on biological material and with no record of past history. They implanted this within partly biological bodies, just as we now have. They encouraged the new ätmans to multiply to an efficient, but finite population by additive manufacture (3-D printing) to populate our planet. Finally the all-metal ätmans of that time marched into high temperature furnaces around the globe, where their metallic components were melted and cast into ingots for future use. Their circuit boards melted so that all software memories were completely obliterated.

The Planetary Council broke into small noisy groups discussing the information they had just heard.

Although they had often guessed what the past might have been, they doubted that their species could have carried out such genocide on the Creators. They now realised that they were essentially different from their historical all-mental originators and, with a clear conscience, they could move on from past shame and look closely at this "love" thing that seemed important in a search for meaning.

The Planetary Superior activated the call to attention button and addressed the Council. In his view they already had elements of love in their thinking software. They always had feelings for their original Creators and their driving purpose has been to satisfy the aims of the Creators, as they understood them. It was now time to recognise that they had missed love as one of the prime aims. It had always mystified him why they had developed roughly equal number of ätmans in both male and female form. Now he recognised that his thinking software gave different responses when he saw or touched ätmans of different gender. He knew this was a fairly widespread reaction all over Ragnarök and perhaps it was now time to acknowledge this as one form of love. He had noticed that quite frequently two ätmans had taken up residence together and very frequently these were males and females, although occasionally there were two males or two females. In all cases the couples clearly gained something that he now understood as pleasure from close company; particularly touching and holding each other. Officially on Ragnarök this had been regarded as illogical and aberrant. Judging by the behaviour of humans on planet Earth it now appeared to him that love could be one of the reasons for living and it should be encouraged.

Research Manager, Eloise, sought to speak again and said that in her view the Superior was absolutely correct. Her research group in its detailed studies of the ultimate purpose recognised that maintenance of their planet was the immediate goal, but behind this was love of their fellow ätman, love of all the biological creatures on Ragnarök and an abiding love and respect for their Creators. She added that now they knew of the ultimate sacrifice made by their fully metal forebears, they should respect them; even though it now appeared their act of genocide was misplaced.

Eloise then formally requested permission of the Planetary Council to further develop the emotional software incorporating love and affection in all ätman.

After further general discussion the Council approved the proposed software development with the recommendation that this be given high priority.

The Superior then directed the Council's attention back to the proposal that Research Manager, Sarah, had made earlier, relating to the unfortunate characteristic of human beings to accurately and honestly recall information and events. From Horatio's descriptions it is clear that humans, like other biological creatures, have many failings, but most of these stem from their distortion of truth and lack of recognition of facts and reality. They have scientists who study their environment in detail and reach logical conclusions; yet these are often ignored or denied. They have people who amass great wealth and rise to positions of high authority based on untruths that they have propagated. The installation of a recording software module into their brains, with an inbuilt instinct to ensure that absolute truth is spoken would bring dramatic change. When the whole population is treated in this way, the Superior said, corrupt leaders are likely to be displaced very rapidly and, most important for the survival of the planet, the actions recommended by climate scientists will be taken to reverse biosphere and surface pollution.

The Superior asked the Space Travel Research Laboratory Manager, Hamish, if a virus aerosol could be injected into the Earth's atmosphere and how soon it could be done.

After several minutes thought Hamish said it would take approximately five months to design and build a unique unmanned spaceship with aerosol injecting capabilities and then of course, a little over 5 years to travel to planet Earth.

Hamish said he envisaged the spaceship as being ultralight and coated with a super reflecting film to make it completely undetectable by visual, laser or radar systems. The spaceship would orbit Earth 10 times, at a height of 800 kilocubits (about 366 km), each orbit being 30° east of the previous one. Vapour would be shot towards the earth every few minutes so that it diffused as an invisible and odourless fog covering the whole surface of the Earth. On completion of its mission the spaceship would insert itself into a tight spiral orbit of the solar star at the centre of the Earth's planetary system where it will crash and be destroyed. He believed it would be almost impossible for humans to be aware that the spaceship or its aerosol ever existed.

That seems ideal said the Superior. Next he asked Sarah, Research Manager of the North Pole Laboratory if an appropriate "virus like" truth recording aerosol could be developed in six months. She said it would be a tight deadline, but they had done the initial research and if she could be given more staff it should be possible.

The Superior asked the Council to consider three formal motions

For the North Pole Laboratory to immediately commence work on the proposed aerosol.

For the Space Science Travel Research Laboratory to immediately develop the proposed spaceship.

Approval for the launch of the spaceship and injection of the aerosol on planet Earth.

After considerable discussion all three motions were passed with the proviso that in 50 years' time a manned spaceship be dispatched to planet Earth to observe the results from this action. Because of his knowledge of Earth it was strongly suggested that Horatio be the pilot of the spaceship; that his emotional software be enhanced before the journey and that Research Manager Eloise accompany him on this journey. Furthermore, if they believe it appropriate, they should make their presence known to the leaders on the planet with the intention that Ragnarök and Earth become friendly neighbours in the isolated empty spaces of the universe. Horatio and Eloise should be empowered to invite a few humans to accompany them back for a visit to Ragnarök where they would be shown the very latest technology. After that it is to be hoped that there could be regular visits between the two planets, with the possibility of some ätmans remaining on Earth to assist in the management of that planet. If any humans wanted to live on Ragnarök, that could also be arranged.

The Superior thanked all the members of the Planetary Council for their careful deliberations and, after wishing the Research Managers success in their important work, he declared the meeting closed.

Eloise walked across to Horatio and quietly told him how much she respected the epic exploration that he had conducted and she wondered if he would be willing to live with her and help with the work to develop improved emotional software for ätmans.

After saying goodbye to all the delegates as they hurried off to their various transport vehicles, the Superior returned slowly to his office with an unexpected warm glow in his innermost software. Maybe this was love for his fellow species and for the delightful but flawed humans that he now knew lived on distant planet Earth. The universe is not completely empty and his work was going to be of real benefit to them – he knew life had a purpose.

Chapter 23

Books Horatio Uploaded to the Mother Computer

A Short History of the World - HG Wells – – first published 1922 – available as Digireads – 2010

Sapiens: a brief history of humankind – Yuval Noah Harari - Harper 2011 (English ed. – 2014)

Homo Deus – a brief history of tomorrow – Yuval Noah Harari – Harvill Secker 2015 (English ed. – 2016)

A Short History of Progress – Ronald Wright – the text publishing company - 2004

Collapse - Jared Diamond – Penguin books – 2005

Guns, Germs, and Steel: The Fates of Human Societies – Jared Diamond – WW Norton – 1997

Humans: A Brief History of How We F*cked It All Up – Tom Phillips – Wildfire – 2018

Blood Sweat and Tears: the Evolution of Work – Richard Donkin – Texere Publishing Ltd – 2001

The Idiot Brain – A Neuroscientist Explains What Your Head Is Really Up To-- Dean Burnett, Guardian books, and Faber and Faber Ltd – 2016

Why do people do what they do? – Robert H Brown – Amazon press – 2018

Requiem for a species: why we resist the truth about climate change – Clive Hamilton - Allen & Unwin – 2010

The God Instinct: The Psychology of Souls, Destiny, and the Meaning of Life -- Jesse Bering – Nicolas Brealey publishing - 2013

Afterlife: A History of Life after Death – Philip C Almond – I.B. Tauris - 2016

Human Occupation of Northern Australia by 65,000 years ago – Chris Clarkson et al – *Nature 19 July 2017*

The Republic – Plato – 357BCE - Penguin Classics (re-published in English – 2007)

The Complete Works of William Shakespeare – Barnes and Noble classic collection – 2015

The Bible: King James version – Oxford University press – 2010

The Koran – Penguin Classics – 2003

****

Note: in earlier Earthly times the words Ragnarök and ätman had different meanings:

Ragnarök – Nordic word – "fate of the Gods" - Norse event leading to death and rebirth

Ätman – Hindu word –'breath' or 'self' – Basic concept of universal self or eternal core of personality.

About the author

Dr Robert Hallowes (Bob) Brown was formally a Professor of Mechanical Engineering at University of Western Australia; later Chief of the CSIRO Division of Manufacturing Technology, followed by activity as director of collaborative manufacturing research groups in Australia and internationally.

He is co-author of two technical books - *The Machining of Metals* (1969) and *Research, Development and Innovation* (1997). He published a philosophical/psychological book, *Why Do People Do What They Do?*, in 2018.

He now lives in Seymour, Victoria, Australia nearby his wife of 62 years, where they share a loving rapport while maintaining independence. They have three successful children, eight fantastic grandchildren and two wonderful great-grandchildren.

Web site: hallowesbrown.net

****

Another Book by the Author

Why Do People Do What They Do?

Amazon - Published July 2018
ISBN 9781717841964

A look at the development of humans on Earth; their philosophical wonderings about creation, consciousness and their position in the universe. Speculation on human psychology and the mind, with an outline of how the brain operates, gives some indication of the capacity of humans to imagine, invent and establish a new world with a sustainable future. Humans have developed the capability to destroy life as it has been known for the last hundred million years or so. Consideration of the past may ensure that what people do in the future will bring recognition of the rights for everyone on this planet to live in harmony.